The best sex is ~~safe~~ *saved* sex.

ALSO BY
DARREN WASHINGTON

MILLIKEN UNIVERSITY
Young Alumni of the Year | 2005

GARY COMMUNITY SCHOOL CORPORATION
School Board Member | Since 2004
School Board President | 2005

ESSENCE MAGAZINE
"Do Right Man" | 2007

DARREN WASHINGTON FOR MAYOR
Candidate for Mayor of Gary | 2007

A *DUMMIES* GUIDE TO
SEXUAL PURITY & DATING

The best sex is ~~safe~~ *saved* sex.

DARREN WASHINGTON

dlw publishing

"Then the Lord said to Cain. "Why are you angry? Why is your face downcast? If you do what is right, will you not be accepted? But if you do not do what is right, sin is crouching at your door; it desires to have you, but you must master it." *Genesis 4:6-7*

Copyright 2009
Written by
Darren L. Washington
A Dummies Guide to Sexual Purity and Dating

Editing by
Chelsea L. Whittington

Creative by
Ami K. Reese

Publisher's Note
Names, characters, places, and incidents either are a product of the author's imagination or are used fictitiously, and any resemblance to actual persons, living or dead, events, or locales is entirely coincidental.

Library of Congress
Cataloging-in-Publication Data
ISBN 10: 0615314120
ISBN 13: 978-0-615-31412-9

Printed in the United States of America

All rights reserved. No part of this book may be reproduced, stored in a retrieval system or transmitted in any form by any means, electronic, mechanical, photocopy, recording or otherwise, without the prior permission of the publisher, except as provided by USA copyright law.

Scripture quotations in this book are taken from the Holy Bible, New International Version®. NIV®. Copyright© 1973, 1978, 1984 by International Bible Society. Used by emission of Zondervan Publishing House. All rights reserved.

Bible quotations marked KJV are taken from the King James Version of the Bible.

Published by
DLW PUBLISHING & PROMOTION
PO Box 892
Gary, IN 46402
darren.washington@sbcglobal.net

BOOK DEDICATION

I thank God for his son and my savior Jesus Christ
and The Power of the Holy Spirit

I dedicate this book to my parents who raised, nurtured,
developed, spanked and loved me with all of their heart

Leonard and Floria Washington

ACKNOWLEDGEMENTS

*To the men whom have
influenced my spiritual growth.*

PASTOR JEFFREY JOHNSON
Eastern Star Church
Indianapolis, Indiana

PASTOR CEDRIC J. OLIVER
Embassies of Christ Church
Gary, Indiana

PASTOR CHRISTOPHER THORPE
New Beginnings Outreach Ministries
Gary, Indiana

"*Prayer is powerful. Don't leave home without it.*"

TABLE OF CONTENTS

PREFACE ... Man Up!!!

FOREWORD ... A Kingdom Mindset

INTRODUCTION

1. YOU ARE ROYALTY

2. DOGGISH MEN ARE NOT BORN, THEY ARE CREATED BY SILLY WOMEN

3. PREGNANT WITH PURPOSE

4. STEPS TO "SAVED SEX"

5. HONESTY IS THE BEST POLICY

6. SEX AND THE CHURCH

7. CONCLUSION: Life Letters and Words of Wisdom

PURITY IS POSSIBLE

"Darren has been passionate in his pursuit of sexual abstinence. His life is an inspiration and role model to many. I know that this book will be a blessing to all that read it, because it is written by one who walks the talk."
PASTOR CEDRIC J. OLIVER
Embassies of Christ Church | Gary, Indiana

"Darren Washington is an outstanding role model for our young people. In this book, he persuasively presents abstinence as a necessary option. One that singles can choose to help promote a healthy and promising future, both emotionally and spiritually."
REVEREND DALE J. MELCZEK
Bishop of the Diocese of Gary

"Out-of-wedlock births constitute 80% of all pregnancies within inner city communities. Darren's strong leadership and commitment will contribute to healthy families."
MITCHELL E. DANIELS, JR.
Governor, State of Indiana

"A Dummies' Guide to Sexual Purity" is a bold and courageous approach in reclaiming Christian values. The book is excellent opposition to popular culture and contains magnificent advice for youth and adult singles who seek to abstain from sex until marriage."
DR. MYRTLE V. CAMPBELL
Superintendent, Gary Community Schools

"Mr. Washington is to be commended for his commitment to his work in the area of abstinence education. He communicates through example that the youth of today can make choices in the way they live their lives. He is an exemplary role model for the future of young adults."
DR. SHARON JOHNSON-SHIRLEY
Superintendent, Lake Ridge Schools

"Darren is just amazing. He came from a non-abstinent lifestyle, to choose secondary virginity and to change the lives of hundreds — perhaps thousands of teens. Darren was able to realize the destructive influence premarital sexual activity had on his life and changed his life."

LESLEE UNRUH
President, Abstinence Clearinghouse

"A Dummies Guide to Sexual Purity" will help men to understand that the key point of finding true love is spiritual not sexual. Abstinence is a true sign of loving and valuing one's self through self control, self love, self discipline and self motivation which leads to a successful person."

RODRICK "LOVE ARCHITECT" GLOVER
President, Motivations Inc. | Nashville, Tennessee

"From sex and the church, to oral sex, to how male dogs are not born but made and the 'silly women' who create them, Darren Washington's, "A Dummies Guide to Sexual Purity and Dating, is the most candid and in your face book I've ever read on this subject. Truly relevant, this book speaks to this generation — where "sexting" with an LOL Smiley face is the norm — and it resonates with teenagers and adults alike while offering real solutions and real alternatives to a promiscuous lifestyle. You can't get any more 'real' than this!"

KIM BROOKS
Author "He's Fine ... But is He Saved?"
and "He's Saved ... But is He For Real?"

PREFACE

MAN UP!!!
One of the greatest controversies debated is the issue of "sexual abstinence and purity.} Isn't sex a human legitimate need? Why marry? What's the big deal about sex before marriage? What is a soul tie? Darren Washington answers these questions.

As a pastor and friend, I have seen him not only talk the talk, but walk the walk. He is a role model to men that you can remain sexually pure until marriage. He is able to relate to youth and single adults who struggle with the issues of sex, singleness and purity. This subject, which is mainly discussed by women, is now being addressed by a single man. Men and women have different needs. The measure of a man is not how many women you can have sex with, but waiting for a wife to make love to. Therefore, I believe men will be challenged by this book to man-up.

Darren has accepted a mandate to go unto the world and teach this important subject within the body of Christ and in the secular world. You will find this book enlightening as he communicates clearly about the traps to avoid. Men will learn that abstinence is not a weakness, and women will appreciate discovering that not all men are dogs.

I challenge churches, pastors, and leaders in the body of Christ not to run away from this subject but embrace it as a reality in our life that must be addressed.

What is the benefit of waiting for sex until marriage? You will find out as you read, and enjoy "A Dummies Guide to Sexual Purity and Dating."

PASTOR CHRIS THORPE
New Beginnings Outreach Ministry
Gary, Indiana

SEX TALK:
THE EXCUSES PEOPLE MAKE

For the purpose of gaining an accurate understanding of how many sexually active people view abstinence, let's see what we're up against.

"Sex feels so good. It's not like I'm having sex with unknown one-night-stands. Besides that, I use protection, what's the big deal?" asked Mr. Anonymous. "What better way to show my love and prove my faithfulness?"

Ms. Anonymous said, "I understand the importance of abstinence, but we have physical needs. I know he loves me, and we're together all the time. I just can't risk losing another relationship, especially when we're going to eventually have sex anyway. I think he's really the one this time."

"I personally feel sorry for people, especially grown men, who haven't had sex," Mr. Anonymous belted out. "It's so unusual that it has to mess with the mind."

"You're crazy! How can anybody marry somebody without having sex with them first?" asked Mr. Anonymous. "That's insane."

"I'm not crazy enough to believe that he's going to actually marry me if we don't have sex." Ms. Anonymous said. "It's simple. he gave me a ring so I'm giving him what he wants. Who cares what other people think?"

"It's not natural to hold back your sexual desires when love is mutual," Mr. Anonymous said. "Sex is natural and meant to be enjoyed."

"I'm a Christian. God is forgiving. I believe in the Bible. I even give tithes to my church. I also participate in midweek services, and I absolutely do not agree with pre-marital sex," Ms. Anonymous said. "But what I do in the privacy of my home is my business. When I slip up and have sex, God forgives that, too."

"People shouldn't be so judgmental of others," Mrs. Anonymous said. "I had sex before I got married, and the world did not come to an end."

"I tried the 'abstinent thing' for about 7-months," he said. "it didn't work because it's not natural."

"Some people pretend to be abstinent because it is more socially acceptable than the lie they're really living," she said. "In other words, they use the term to conceal the truth about their alternative lifestyle."

"We look at it this way. if you use protection, sex is safe," a college couple agreed. "We're far too young to even think about marriage, please!"

"How can we talk to our children about abstaining from sex until marriage, if we had sex before marriage?" Mr. and Mrs. Parents said. "We just hope and pray our girls won't get pregnant."

"She is so fine, and we met at church," Mr. Anonymous said. "She's a great cook, and in the bedroom, Lord! I know what we are doing is wrong, but I, I just can't let her go."

"I gave that woman my love, body and money, and she dumped me for another man that treated her like crap. I'm going to have sex with as many women as possible to get her out of my mind."

"Hey, I have material needs, and that was explained to him when we got together. When I don't get what I want, I hold out until he pay's up."

"I got this disease because he was living on the Down Low! I hate men, and I want to make sure as many of them feel what I'm feeling right now!"

FOREWORD

A KINGDOM MINDSET

Sexual Purity and abstinence are two concepts that often are used interchangeably. One cannot have sexual purity without practicing abstinence. The dictionary defines abstinence as "The act or practice of refraining from or indulging an appetite or desire." The Word of God boldly declares in I Thessalonians 5:22 to, "Abstain from all appearance of evil." The appearance of evil would be a visible outward expression to one or many. By the time an evil thought is made visible through an outward expression, the thought has gone through a process. This process always starts in the mind! Our minds are fertile, always looking for something to stimulate itself.

There are so many things that affect our mind, and the decisions that we ultimately make. Television has an influence on our mind. What we see visually affects our thoughts, and our thoughts govern our actions. What are you putting in front of your eyes?

Furthermore, what we hear affects our mind. Never before in history has music contained such desecrating lyrics about women. Some might say they are listening to the beat, or they like the voice of the singer and are not paying attention to the words. However, the mind is paying attention! Your mind is receiving and retaining these explicit words. Sooner or later these words and thoughts will make an outward manifestation. So what are you listening to?

Your circle of friends, influence your mind in both of these areas whether you like it or not. You are affected by their ideals and morals whether good or bad. They can influence you by their actions and words. This is exactly what happened to Amnon in the following biblical account:

And it came to pass after this, that Absalom the son of David had a fair sister, whose name [was] Tamar; and Amnon the son of David loved her.

And Amnon was so vexed, that he fell sick for his sister Tamar; for she [was] a virgin; and Amnon thought it hard for him to do anything to her. But Amnon had a friend, whose name [was] Jonadab, the son of Shimeah David's brother: and Jonadab [was] a very subtil man. And he said unto him, Why [art] thou, [being] the king's son, lean from day to day? Wilt thou not tell me? And Amnon said unto him, I love Tamar, my brother Absalom's sister. And Jonadab said unto him, Lay thee down on thy bed, and make thyself sick: and when thy father cometh to see thee, say unto him, I pray thee, let my sister Tamar come, and give me meat, and dress the meat in my sight, that I may see [it], and eat [it] at her hand. So Amnon lay down, and made himself sick: and when the king was come to see him, Amnon said unto the king, I pray thee, let Tamar my sister come, and make me a couple of cakes in my sight, that I may eat at her hand. *II Samuel 13:1-6 KJV*

Amnon was the son of King David, and Tamar was the daughter of King David. A relationship with half brothers and sisters was acceptable during this time. Amnon desired to be with Tamar with all his might. His intentions for Tamar were pure, as he truly loved her. The Bible says that he was so vexed for Tamar that he fell sick for her, for she was a virgin. Amnon had principles; he was raised in his Father's house. He was taught to fear the Lord and to obey the teachings of God in so much that Amnon thought it hard to do anything sexual to Tamar. There was certainly a battle going on in the mind of Amnon.

This battle was one that he fought for a long period of time, and he was winning. In spite of his urges, it was hard for him to do anything to Tamar. But Amnon had a friend! His name was Jonadab, and he was a very wise man. He observed that something was bothering Amnon and inquired about his problem. After hearing Amnon's story, Jonadab devised a plan to get Amnon what he wanted. That was to get Amnon alone with Tamar, so he could be intimate with her. His friend delivered the ultimate blow to his mind. Amnon heard the words of Jonadab and put the plan into motion. What kind of friends do you have?

Purity begins in the mind, travels to your heart and shows forth through your actions. Abstinence is more than just saying, "NO." It is a lifestyle of purity that begins in your mind. The Bible states "Let this mind be in you, which was also in Christ Jesus." *Philippians 2:5 KJV*

In this book, I believe that you will find advice to men and women that will help you win the battle of sexual purity. I don't ask for you to agree with it all, but simply think about what is written. Darren Washington has given us a tool to win this battle; and through the Lord Jesus Christ, we CAN live an overcoming life. Enjoy this book, and share it with others.

PASTOR PHIL ENDRIS
The Rock Church
Gary, Indiana

INTRODUCTION

One of the most consequential trends of our time is the dramatic increase in the number of children growing up in fatherless households. I thank God for the many faithful and fearless single mothers and fathers who for many years have effectively raised their children.

Pre-marital sex is one of the leading causes of single-parent households in our society, and innocent children ultimately suffer. The absence of either parent often leads to various adolescent dysfunctions. When many of these children mature into adults, they remain in denial while burying their vulnerabilities deep within. There are many other consequences when giving in to pre-marital sex including sexually transmitted diseases and emotional/spiritual damage. These issues often affect suburban, rural or inner-city families.

In economically suppressed communities, there are overwhelming percentages of households with single-mothers. Love-struck women seldom receive long-term support from deceptive men seeking short-term pleasure. Outside of introducing someone to Jesus Christ, your body is the greatest gift you can give someone.

After most people have their first sexual experience, they convince themselves that they can't stop. Some people don't want to abstain from sex thinking being cool and gaining acceptance with the "in-crowd" is more important. Many teenagers are trapped into believing that something is wrong or abnormal about virginity. Actually, something is wrong with people who sell their self-worth for a few minutes of ecstasy.

You can abstain from sex until marriage! *A Dummy's Guide to Sexual Purity and Dating* will change the way you think and provide the steps necessary to help you abstain. Your individual decision to abstain until marriage will make you a trendsetter. You will be empowered with a greater sense of self-worth, a more promising future, and a greater value of individual identity. Abstaining from sex until marriage also contributes to a more promising and respectable society.

Childbirth makes mothers trendsetters by nature, and a woman's body is the greatest gift she could give a man. Avoiding sex before marriage sets the kind of positive trends that build moral fibers within communities. Women have always been an invisible foundation, neglected resource, and a misunderstood power. Every mother whether married or single is worthy of a certain degree of honor. Unfortunately, single-parenting raises multiple concerns that are discussed throughout this book.

Male or female, your body is one of the most valuable gifts you can give to anyone. It's no secret that most young girls share the fairy tale of saving themselves for the man of their dreams. Unfortunately, this seldom happens because even so-called "good women" are exchanging sex for commitment. The women, who surrender their "goods" too soon, are often viewed as whores, easy and, at best, "old news". In our own senseless and silent way of communicating, men deem waiting as something worthwhile, especially if he realizes the value of human worth. Immature men won't acknowledge your worth unless you do. Others will identify your weakness as a means to get what they want. Most women desperately want to feel loved. As a result, a few flowers, dinners, late-night phone conversations, and one softly spoken "I love you," often leads to lust fulfilled sex before marriage.

A woman's body is one of the most precious gifts she could give a man. Real men, mature men, Godly spiritual men, understand that sex is worth waiting for. Challenge your friends to step on the stage and dare to be different by practicing abstinence until marriage. It's not easy being a trendsetter, but by doing so, you'll possess the power to positively change society.

We must teach younger men and remind older men that sexual gratification is not a measure of manhood, and that all females must be treated like respected queens, regardless of their outward demeanor and behavior. Men must also understand in the midst of conflict, controversy and confusion it does not make you less of a man to walk away.

I've been teaching the message of sexual abstinence and purity for 15 years. Now that I'm 39 years old, I realize even more, the importance of investing in prevention. Our society is slowly reacting to problems caused by sexual promiscuity. We need to become aggressively preventive. It's time to teach and express to all single adults and youth how to put down the condoms and practice self-control. The best option for singles is to strive for a lifestyle of abstinence.

Sex is a billion dollar industry, and it has a negative effect in the way males and females view one another and the way we view ourselves. As a result of this distorted self-image, broken families and relationships are often created. Sexually explicit media propaganda indirectly can encourage abortions, single-parent homes, pornography addition, infidelity and other misfortunes that decay the backbone of America – the family structure.

We have too many people receiving on-the-job training, as it relates to marriage. In other words, singles are engaging in the same sexual activities as married couples. Sex before marriage causes single men and some women to ask, "Why get married?" During the dating stages of relationships, investing in friendships and not engaging in sexual activity before marriage are important. Waiting is the best way to help keep a clear mind while making critical assessments of the benefits and liabilities of a future spouse. Despite how pleasurable, marriages cannot survive on sex alone. This notion has contributed to the more than 50-percent divorce rate in America.

In addition to sexually transmitted diseases and unplanned pregnancies, there are other issues that pre-marital sex can cause. It's an irresponsible disservice to overlook the emotional, psychological, and spiritual damage. It's easy to find someone who has experienced a broken heart or angry feelings as a result of being used sexually. Some people are wounded so deeply that it affects their daily behavior and future relationships. Lust should never be mistaken for love. Never be deceived into hoping that sexual favors will result in marriage. It's considered manipulation when having sex to emotionally force someone into marriage. It's prostitution when having sex with someone to obtain material possessions and/or money.

Abstinence alone will not prevent a broken heart, but will prevent sexually transmitted diseases and unwanted pregnancy. God created sex for the marriage covenant only. Women, a commitment is only worthy of sex after he stands before the pastor, priest, or judge and seal with the promise of "I do."

Parents must become more responsible in teaching the benefits of sexual abstinence and the pitfalls of sex before marriage to their children. Many parents feel because of their past engagement in pre-marital sex, it would seem hypocritical to teach sexual abstinence to their children. God is not as concerned with your past as He is with your possibilities. Your past mistakes can serve as one of the best sexual abstinence lessons in helping your child become a positive trendsetter.

Our churches must become more active in teaching singles about all aspects of sexual activity. I would encourage all churches to invest into their single ministries as they do their youth ministries. There are many singles who are struggling with sexual sin for different reasons, and the church must open its arms with love and start assisting with the healing process.

As single individuals, no matter our age, race or gender, we must be responsible in promoting abstinence awareness. This will help to prevent future generations from having to deal with some of the social ills our society is currently facing. If you are serious about living a life of sexual purity until marriage, this book will help. In part, the future of your family and our society will depend on the spouse that you choose. That choice must be made without the contamination of premarital sex.

Until men and women begin working together for the sake of the family structure, there will continue to be a rise in teen pregnancies, single-parenting, deadbeat dads, abortions, welfare recipients, financial burdens and countless other socioeconomic ills. Unfortunately, until we learn the value of self control and sexual abstinence, men and women will continue shifting the blame in a proverbial "battle of the sexes."

Despite the past, people can change. Sometimes, you must allow people to change from a distance in order to promote growth. Don't allow anyone or any circumstance cause you to believe that you can't become a better person. You can! Perhaps you've already lost your virginity, had an abortion or contracted a sexually transmitted disease. It's still not too late to start over! We are covered by the blood of Jesus Christ.

Sexual Abstinence is an action, but Sexual Purity is a lifestyle. Sexual abstinence is refraining from sex, and the cause can be for multiple reasons. Sexual Purity is a lifestyle, and the reason for abstaining is to help build a better relationship with God. A person can abstain and cheat in a relationship, abstain and be unforgiving, abstain and be hateful, prideful, slothful, to name a few. Purity is the condition or quality of being free from anything that debases, contaminates, and pollutes. Sex outside of marriage has been the cause of many societal problems. We must become serious about our relationship with God. Through prayer, study and action, God has a desire to do great things through us.

Today marks a new beginning in your life. No matter what you've done in the past, you can become a positive trendsetter. The perfect beginning in an imperfect world is building a better you!

CHAPTER ONE

YOU ARE ROYALTY

"Therefore if any man be in Christ, he is a new creature: old things are passed away; behold, all things are become new."

2 CORINTHIANS 5:17 KJV

For the past fifteen years, I have been spreading the message of sexual abstinence in public schools, colleges, universities, churches and in my community. I realized a long time ago why many single people engage in sexual relationships before marriage. Many of us don't know who we are, forget who we are and, at times, ignore who we are in order to feed our selfish desires. By accepting Jesus Christ as my Lord and Savior, I have been able to live a lifestyle of sexual abstinence and purity. I also fear God and the consequences of choosing to live a sinful lifestyle.

Federal and most state governments have provided organizations and institutions with funding to spread the message of sexual abstinence before marriage. These initiatives are much needed to combat the rise in teen pregnancy and the spreading of viral and non-viral sexually transmitted diseases. It is also taught that pre-marital sex can result in negative emotional consequences. The obstacle in teaching the emotional side of sexual abstinence in public schools is that the Word of God is not allowed. The scripture is the only way for us to get a clear understanding of the emotional and spiritual consequences of sex outside of marriage.

In my experience of speaking, teaching and counseling, I have found that youth must hear the message of abstinence and purity in order to assist them in making the correct choices concerning sexual activity for the rest of their lives. Youth eventually become single adults. Many become married adults, and many in both groups become parents. Single adults need to be taught the message of sexual abstinence as are our youth. No matter what age range you fall into, if you are single you should not be engaging in sexual relationships before marriage.

As the singles ministry leader of my church in Gary, Indiana, I am convinced that all church single ministries should focus on preparing singles to be ministry focused "God Chasers." When you ask a single person "Why do you want to be married?" Many singles will say "It's time to settle down," "I want to have children," or "I want to be with that special person." Marriage is a ministry to glorify God, and carry out his ministry for the Kingdom. Singles must prepare for marriage during their single lives. We need to be in order emotionally, spiritually, financially, and physically before we think about becoming "one flesh" with another person. We have too many people getting "on-the-job-training" when it comes to marriage. If you have the gift of celibacy for the rest of your life, that's fine, but most people don't. I'm preparing for my mighty woman of God! Married couples can help singles understand the expectations and responsibilities of marriage.

To be honest, there is a great need for more men to come out and assume their assignments as leaders and teachers in our churches and communities. Specifically speaking, we need strong, married men speaking and serving as living examples of the benefits of marriage. A lot of men are running from marriage like Olympic sprinters. Others are getting married thinking it will cure their "doggish" mentality, and some say "I do" because of sex. We need more single men speaking out on the importance of sexual abstinence and purity.

Men need to speak to young men and adult single men about the benefit of abstinence and staying pure for their potential woman of God. Men also need to speak to women about the importance of staying pure for their potential man of God. The message of abstinence coming from either man or woman is good. However, the meaning, desire and perception of sex vary because our gender makeup is different. Boys, girls, single men and women will all react differently to the message of sexual abstinence because needs and designs are different.

INTIMACY WITH GOD

The message of sexual abstinence is so controversial because it is in constant and direct conflict with the world's view of sex and love. Sex is a wonderful activity created by God, only to be exercised in the context of marriage. God designed sex for three reasons:
1. To procreate the human race
2. To seal the blood covenant between male and female
3. For enjoyment without repercussions
   (in the context of marriage)

When a person makes a decision to give their life to God and become a Christian, he or she will soon begin to wrestle within. When we give our life to God, we come to him on different levels, with different struggles and wanting to change for the better. To begin the intervention process we must renew our minds because the journey will not be easy.

"Do not conform any longer to the pattern of this world, but be transformed by the renewing of your mind. Then you will be able to test and approve what God's will is — his good, pleasing and perfect will."
Romans 12:2

When you begin to read and study the Word of God on a daily basis, it becomes clear how much God really loves us: Then God said,

"Let us make man in our image, in our likeness, and let them rule over the fish of the sea and the birds of the air, over the livestock, over all the earth, [a] and over all the creatures that move along the ground." 27 So

God created man in his own image, in the image of God he created him; male and female he created them." Genesis 1:26-27

As males and females, we are created in God's image and his likeness. This makes us children of God, and His children are royalty. When you are a child of a king, you must be very careful with whom you associate, with. Spend time with people who are like-minded, respect and live by the word of your king. Prior to becoming male and female, God created Man as a spirit to fellowship with Him because God is a spirit. The "houses" that God created for "Spirit Man" to dwell in are temples named "Male" and "Female." Male and female both have the "Spirit Man" inside their temple, but each temple is designed with a different purpose. Each temple has equal access to God in order to develop a spiritual relationship with Him.

Male was created first by God from the earth, and female was made by God from a rib taken out of the male. I offer this history to explain that the love God has for us as "spirit man" is intended to be expressed and reflected through the relationship between male and female here on earth. God also created men and women to dominate the earth together, not dominate one another. We are one. Woman was made from man, and man is birth out of woman. What a perfect combination.

God is expecting us to build and strengthen our relationship with him. Many of us seek God when we want something or are in trouble. When we don't get the expected results, we get angry with God. If I asked a mighty woman of God to marry me after going on one date, she would look at me as if I were crazy. I haven't proven myself worthy of being her husband, and for her to say "yes" would make her just as silly. God wants to do so much for us because he loves us, but we must build an intimate relationship with Him, not the church. How can you build that relationship?

- Talk to God daily
- Worship and praise God daily
- Read God's Word daily
- Live through the application of God's Word daily
- Let God in on everything about you; make him your confidant
- God is not expecting a performance-based relationship with you
- Praise, worship and love God because He is God (not because of what He can do for you)

God spoke to my mind and heart informing me that having faith to live an effective lifestyle of sexual purity can only come through the Holy Spirit with a belief in Jesus Christ. Sexual abstinence is an action, but sexual purity is a lifestyle. There are people who are sexually abstinent that don't believe in Jesus Christ. The Lord has a desire to have an intimate relationship with us. He wants nothing but the best for us and nothing short of a "kingdom lifestyle." As men and women of God, we need an uninterrupted flow of access to our Lord and Savior so He can direct us in every aspect of our lives. We can't access kingdom living without an intimate relationship with God. We have allowed so many things to keep us away from God. It is time to get serious and be about our Father's business by bringing in the harvest through faith and works. Many of us don't talk about sexual purity, because we are not living sexually pure.

"Do you not know that your bodies are members of Christ himself? Shall I then take the members of Christ and unite them with a prostitute? Never! 16 Do you not know that he who unites himself with a prostitute is one with her in body? For it is said, "The two will become one flesh." 17 But he who unites himself with the Lord is one with him in spirit. 18 Flee from sexual immorality. All other sins a man commits are outside his body, but he who sins sexually sins against his own body. 19 Do you not know that your body is a temple of the Holy Spirit, who is in you, whom you have received from God? You are not your own; 20 You were bought at a price. Therefore honor God with your body. 1 Corinthians 6:15-20

    Earlier, I shared how God created man as a spirit, and created two separate houses (male and female) where "Spirit Man" would dwell. This passage warns us about the seriousness of sexual immorality and the spiritual damage it can cause in our lives. Not only do you sin against your own body, but you begin to slowly close the door of intimacy with God. One of the reasons that sex was created for the marriage covenant was to allow sex to be enjoyed without repercussions. God knew the soul ties, sexual perversion, disease, death and family breakdown that would be created as a result of sex outside of marriage. Many of us who have had sexual relationships in the past can remember the pain and problems we faced because of our disobedience. We also know of the battle within due to instant pleasure from past sexual behavior. Until marriage, our obligation is to be faithful to God. If you can't be faithful to God, how can you be faithful to your spouse? We are married in our singleness.

    No person or a few minutes of sexual activity is worth jeopardizing your intimate relationship with God. You and your future spouse should not have to compete with the sexual performances of past partners. Begin today by living in the spirit and not giving in to the desire of the flesh. As you begin to develop a closer, intimate relationship with God, the desires of the sinful nature will test you to see how solid you stand on the word of God.

"So I say live by the Spirit and you will not gratify the desires of the sinful nature. 17 For the sinful nature desires what is contrary to the Spirit and the Spirit what is contrary to the sinful nature. They are in conflict with each other, so that you do not do what you want. 18 But if you are led by the Spirit, you are not under law. 19 The acts of the sinful nature are obvious: sexual immorality, impurity and debauchery; 20 idolatry and witchcraft; hatred, discord, jealousy, fits of rage, selfish ambition, dissensions, faction's 21 and envy; drunkenness, orgies, and the like. I warn you, as I did before, that those who live like this will not inherit the kingdom of God. 22 But the fruit of the Spirit is love, joy, peace, patience, kindness, goodness, faithfulness, 23 gentleness and self-control. Against such things there is no law. 24 Those who belong to Christ Jesus have crucified the sinful nature with its passions and desires." Galatians 5:16-24

Sexual immorality is not the only thing we must be concerned with when trying to live in the will of God. God is not expecting us to be perfect, but he does want us to depend on Him 100% of the time to get through our struggles. The greatest gift we received from God outside of Jesus Christ was free will. If you have already made a commitment or are thinking about being sexually pure, I can personally attest that it was the best choice I ever made as a man. I have been able to improve in all areas of my life not only in being sexually abstinent.

Choosing a spouse is one of the most important decisions we will ever make. We must depend on God so He can assist us in choosing our future mate. A large percentage of the struggles and successes in our married lives will depend on the choices we make while single. We need to improve our lives in all areas in order to access the Kingdom of God. He has so much to show and share with us. When you choose to live for God, you will be tested by satan. God will never leave or forsake you! You must be tested in order to prove that the Word of God is true. The Word of God will prepare you for a lifetime of tests.

1 Corinthians 10:12-13 12 So, if you think you are standing firm, be careful that you don't fall! 13No temptation has seized you except what is common to man. And God is faithful; he will not let you be tempted beyond what you can bear. But when you are tempted, he will also provide a way out so that you can stand up under it.

THE BIGGEST LOSER

How many of us are willing to lose everything, die out to our will and submit to the will of God? Are we willing to die to sinful behavior, selfish desires and to our own successes to please God? Taking this approach allows us to grow closer to the will of God and enables us to access His Kingdom. Are you willing to die out to having pre-marital sex, drugs, impurity, selfish ambition, envy, drunkenness, back biting, discord, jealousy, not tithing and any other thing that has prevented you from having an intimate relationship with God?

Matthew 10:38-39 38and anyone who does not take his cross and follow me is not worthy of me. 39Whoever finds his life will lose it, and whoever loses his life for my sake will find it.

When we make the decision to follow God's will and not our own, there will be some people who will not understand our change. Some may be good friends, family and church members and even enemies. In order to be worthy of God, we must take up our personal cross and follow Him through the Garden of Gethsemane. I express this not to scare you, but to guide you through seed time and harvest. Just because you give your live to Christ doesn't mean that in seven days you will get a major harvest. Giving money to the church does not guarantee that you will become rich. It takes time for seeds to grow into a harvest. What are you going to do while you are waiting on your harvest? My advice is to engage in consistent prayer, study the Word, live the Word and have faith in the Word.

Isaiah 40:31 31But they that wait upon the LORD shall renew their strength; they shall mount up with wings as eagles; they shall run, and not be weary; and they shall walk, and not faint.

One of the best shows on television that compares to seed time, death and harvest is "The Biggest Loser." The program focuses on a group of individuals who have made the decision to make some major changes in their lives concerning their weight, eating habits and other things that may have caused them to miss out on God's blessings. Think of all the things we have tried to lose or die out to in our daily lives. It's not an easy process. It takes time, dedication, focus and most of all, belief that through Jesus Christ who strengthens us, all things are possible. The problem is that many of us give up too soon in the midst of seed development (the process) in our lives.

Are you good ground? An intimate relationship with God can keep you focused during this time. satan's goal is to distract you from the promises of God, and the harvest will not grow over night. Please do not give up your prize while going through the process.

Mark 4:3-20 3"Listen! A farmer went out to sow his seed. 4As he was scattering the seed, some fell along the path, and the birds came and ate it up. 5Some fell on rocky places, where it did not have much soil. It sprang up quickly, because the soil was shallow. 6But when the sun came up, the plants were scorched, and they withered because they had no root. 7Other seed fell among thorns, which grew up and choked the plants, so that they did not bear grain. 8Still other seed fell on good soil. It came up, grew and produced a crop, multiplying thirty, sixty, or even a hundred times." 9Then Jesus said, "He who has ears to hear, let him hear." 10When he was alone, the Twelve and the others around him asked him about the parables. 11He told them, "The secret of the kingdom of God has been given to you. But to those on the outside everything is said in parables 12so that, 'they may be ever seeing but never perceiving, and ever hearing but never understanding; otherwise they might turn and be forgiven! 13Then Jesus said to them, "Don't you understand this parable? How then will you understand any parable? 14The farmer sows the word. 15Some people are like seed along the path, where the word is sown. As soon as they hear it, satan comes and takes away the word that was sown in them. 16Others, like seed sown on rocky places, hear the word and at once receive it with joy. 17But since they have no root, they last only a short time. When trouble or persecution comes because of the word, they quickly fall away. 18Still others, like seed sown among thorns, hear the word; 19but the worries of this life, the deceitfulness of wealth and the desires for other things come in and choke the word, making it unfruitful. 20Others, like seed sown on good soil, hear the word, accept it, and produce a crop—thirty, sixty or even a hundred times what was sown."

I love this passage of scripture because Jesus provides us with information in this parable to help us understand how to access the Kingdom of God. In order to truly understand this passage, you must use your spiritual eyes to read, understand, believe and then act on God's instructions. As stated earlier in this chapter, these are steps towards intimacy with God's that will allow you to reap the benefits of His Kingdom.

Many of us have experienced this passage concerning seed time and harvest in regards to finances. Many Christians hear the message "sow your seed (money) to God and reap a harvest (money)" but seldom do we hear about the struggle of patience and the trials of the Garden of Gethsemane we must travel through to get to the harvest. "Harvest" is not limited to financial blessings. When you allow the Word of God to grow within, it will take some time to see results. We will never be allowed to feed on the Word of God continuously without being tested. Again, I ask, are you good ground?

A contestant on "The Biggest Loser" makes a major decision to plant the seed of living in divine health just as a person would make the decision to start living by the Word of God. As a Christian begins to study the Word of God, the contestant begins to study how to live and what actions to take to assist in their weight transformation. When Christians begin to study the Word of God and hear it preached, we often get fired up about His promises. The contestant is also getting fired up because he or she visualizes the end result of a new beautiful body and the benefits that result from weighing 30, 60, 90 or even 120 pounds less. The Christian and the contestant must go through a process to obtain their rewards. The type and length of the process is up to God. We have no control. We must not give up when we don't see quick results remembering that God is not on our time, we are on His.

Mark 4:26-29 26He also said, "This is what the kingdom of God is like. A man scatters seed on the ground. 27Night and day, whether he sleeps or gets up, the seed sprouts and grows, though he does not know how. 28All by itself the soil produces grain—first the stalk, then the head, then the full kernel in the head. 29As soon as the grain is ripe, he puts the sickle to it, because the harvest has come."

Are you like seed along the path? Do you hear the word of God at church and have no intentions of living a life pleasing to God? satan distracts you with no struggle and takes your seed as soon as you hear it. You know it's wrong to have sex before marriage, but it's too good to give up. You my friend are seed that fell along the path. Some contestants, when finding out that they must eat balanced low calorie meals and exercise, leave the show. Others are only interested in getting 15 minutes of fame. Still other contestants knew from the beginning that they were not going to have enough will power to complete the challenge.

Are you like seed sown on rocky places? You get fired up when you hear the message of living for God although you've been "slipping" and "dipping." It has been a struggle, but you have been doing okay for the last month. The contestant is also doing okay, but for the past couple of weeks, this lifestyle change in diet and exercise has been a struggle for them as well. When the enemy is allowed to test these individuals, they quickly fall away because they have no root. We must allow time for seed (Word of God) to grow in our soil to begin the harvest process. When you get tempted to have sex with someone, you give in to loneliness and lust. You get tired of waiting and fighting the challenge of sexual abstinence. This is a result of not allowing the word (seed) to grow in your life.

Because of the exercise, the contestant's body is hurting in ways he or she never thought possible and they are always hungry due to the change in their diet. People begin to tell them it's impossible to change and lose the weight. Ultimately, they leave the show not allowing the root of a healthy lifestyle to grow within and eventually reap their harvest of healthy weight loss. There are some things you must be willing to go through to reap your harvest. The Lord will never take you away from something if He did not have something better for you. The God we serve would never take something out of us if he were not going to put something better in us.

Are you like seed sown among thorns? You hear the word of God, but the worries of this life, deceitfulness of wealth and selfish desires come in and choke the word of God making it unfruitful or unbelievable to you. When you don't see the harvest coming as fast as you think it should, you allow certain things to choke the Word. For example, you haven't dated in a year and worry about being single for the rest of your life so you make an unwise sexual decision. Perhaps you use your physical attributes or sex appeal to climb the corporate ladder because you can't wait on God's method of promotion. You may use someone for your own selfish desires without regard to their emotions by making promises you don't intend to keep. Similarly, the contestant becomes worried and gives up on losing weight because he or she has not seen any results in the first two weeks of diet and exercise. They have desires to go back to the old eating habits because this mountain seems impossible to climb.

Are you like seed sown among good soil? When you begin reading, studying and living the Word of God, you are developing your soil as good ground so that seeds can grow and be rooted. When you hear the Word, accept it and live it, your harvest develops. The decision to take up your cross and follow Jesus will, at times, present difficulties, but we can do all things through Jesus Christ who strengthens us. Depending on God during trials and difficult times will benefit you. Reading and studying the Word of God will enable you to choose the correct man or woman of God for you. Prayer for wisdom and discernment will also guide you in making better decisions concerning dating and relationships.

I don't care how good your soil, seed will never grow without rain. Sometimes the rain will be a drizzle, light, heavy, or a storm, but rain is required for growth. When it begins to rain, please don't give up. The Lord must allow us to be tested to see if we actually believe the word we claim to read, study, and hear. Stay focused, because rain and storms don't last forever.

Do you want intimacy with God? If so, it's available. One contestant was able to win "The Biggest Loser" and reap the harvest of a new body, new attitude and improved physical health. As I write, I am also speaking and preaching to myself because I would never encourage others to go through something that I have never experienced myself. I hope you understand that one of our main responsibilities as a Christian is to help spread the gospel of Jesus Christ. This book is not about me, and becoming a Christian is not only about you. Everything is about using our God-given gifts and talents to help advance His Kingdom.

Matthew 9:35-38 35Jesus went through all the towns and villages, teaching in their synagogues, preaching the good news of the kingdom and healing every disease and sickness. 36When he saw the crowds, he had compassion on them, because they were harassed and helpless, like sheep without a shepherd. 37Then he said to his disciples, "The harvest is plentiful but the workers are few. 38 Ask the Lord of the harvest, therefore, to send out workers into his harvest field."

CHAPTER TWO

DOGGISH MEN ARE CREATED BY SILLY WOMEN

Oh yeah I've got trouble with my friends
Trouble in my life
Problems when you don't come home at night
But when you do you always start a fight
But I can't be alone, I need you to come on home
I know you messing around, but who the hell else
is gonna hold me down
Ooooh I gotta be out my mind to think it's gonna work this time
A part of me wants to leave, but the other side still believes

And it kills me to know how much I really love you
So much I wanna ooh hoo ohh to you hoo hoo
Should I grab his cell, call this chick up
Start some shhhh then hang up
Or I should I be a lady
Oohh maybe 'cause I wanna have his babies
Ohh yah yahh 'cause I don't wanna be alone
I don't need to be on my own

MELANIE FIONA
Lyrics "It Kills Me"

"A wife of noble character who can find? She is worth far more than rubies. Her husband has full confidence in her and lacks nothing of value. She brings him good, not harm, all the days of her life." (Proverbs 31:10-12)

Beautiful women come in all shapes, sizes and different levels of wisdom and knowledge. Unfortunately, unhealthy choices are what many of them share in common. Regardless of how perfect a man appears to be during the initial weeks of dating, get to know his character. The first question you should ask a man who is pursuit of your heart is "What is God's purpose for your life?" Get to know his inner circle of friends, and use careful observation. Look for consistencies. Some men play a good game to get what they want. Some women are self-serving as well, but that's the subject of another great book. Nonetheless, everybody wants something. The question is, "Do they want a healthy lasting relationship with you or sex?" There is no such thing as a "no strings" relationship. We all want something, and that something may be good or bad.

Don't act desperate. That's exactly what makes it easier for the next dog to take advantage of you. Have you ever noticed how certain women go from dogs to users, cruelty to abuse and cheaters to outright male whores and players? Women must realize that being alone does not mean living life lonely. Women, who think all men are dogs, should change their taste in men. Take some time to heal. Identify the mistakes that led to your disappointment, and then move on. These types of sexual predators prey on women who are emotionally wounded, especially those in denial. If you've been hurt, accept it. Stop lying to yourself and everybody else. The truth will set you free. Admit your frustration, and get over it. Take some time to focus on yourself. Never forget what you deserve, and then approach dating with the attitude that you're a rare diamond waiting to be discovered. This perspective causes men to respect women or keep stepping. All men are not "dogs," and the good ones are looking for worthwhile women who know their own value.

Men aren't born with "doggish" traits. They are created by silly, lustful or lonely women. Although some females get upset at the mentioning of this, it remains true. Perhaps it seems that I am shifting the blame of failed relationships onto women. I am not. As a responsible man, I am sharing the secrets that boys use to manipulate girls. Their most frequently used weapon is a woman's wounded heart. It's reality whether you like it or not. Silly women always harbor some form of hatred, resentment or anger towards somebody. Once a dog identifies your area of weakness, he makes his approach. He listens. He understands. He agrees. Finally, he has you where he wants you-- feeling understood. Silly women make the game simple for doggish men. You toss the bone, and he moves in for the catch.

A man cannot give you happiness, especially if you are not already happy with yourself. When most women reach their late twenties, and especially thirties, they focus on one primary goal – marriage. Hopefully, this message will speak to your heart. Sexual Purity is much more than just saying "no" to pre-marital sex. Whether single or married, be the best person you can be. This starts with the kind of self-fulfillment that comes from within. The best ways to prepare for a healthy marriage are to learn to love yourself and to be content with your own identity. This will also promote lasting relationships. If you are not content with yourself, be it your economic situation, physical appearance, lack of companionship, where you live, how you live, or education, another person cannot give you that fulfillment. Unhappy people always argue and find fault with others because they're miserable about something unresolved within. People who love life have a pleasant way of drawing others into their world without manipulation. People, who are dissatisfied with their own lives, disconnect themselves, find faults and/or judge others. When you see the need for change, it must begin in you. When you learn to love yourself, it is easier for someone else to love you.

You must remain in control of your life, by the choices you make. You have complete power as it relates to the choices you make. Men can't force you into dating or marriage, the choice is yours. It is important that you choose carefully. One bad choice can cause you a lifetime of heartache and pain. This is one of many reasons why fathers serve critical roles in their daughter's lives. Statistics show that women generally choose men based on their relationship they have or do not have with their fathers. While it's true that sons need fathers, it is an equal reality for daughters. The mere presence of a protective father fosters the kind of security that causes children to feel safe and thereby flourish. We have too many women trying to operate as both mom and dad. There is no such thing as a female dad. The plight of single mothers, teen pregnancies, and deadbeat dads is a major proponent in the breakdown of the family structure, which has impacted countless urban areas.

Avoid people who don't share your core values. A stable and strong family structure depends on the approach taken toward belief systems.

Never compromise your values to be with someone for the sake of companionship. Remember, you can do badly all by yourself. I'll use myself as an example. I am a Christian. I would not date a non-Christian woman who has not accepted Jesus Christ as her savior. I don't care how beautiful she is, how much money she has, or how fast she makes my heart beat. I need a woman who loves Jesus Christ more than she loves me. Her actions would show me how much she loves Jesus Christ. We need people in our lives that will remain strong in the Lord when we get weak and want to make ungodly choices. This standard is based on my belief system. This biblical approach builds a strong marital foundation. If his or her lifestyle contradicts with your beliefs, turn around, run and don't look back! If you allow yourself to get involved in this type of relationship, be prepared for a lifetime of frustration or divorce.

Ask yourself, "Why do I want to be married?" and "What do I value most in a potential spouse?" Women who don't realize what they're looking for are exactly what doggish men want – confused prey roaming aimlessly. Most people, especially those living single lifestyles, get confused between wants and needs. As a result, we compromise our true needs for selfish physical desires. Personal preferences can pose dilemmas in dating. However, finding a spouse is not like buying a car – no test drives! As singles we sometimes search for popularity, good looks, sex appeal, stylish cars, wealth and other material possessions. It's not sin to want a good-looking spouse with financial blessings. Don't allow the love for the material and physical cause you to make the choice to live outside of the will of God. Now that the difference between "wants" and "needs" has been identified, ask yourself again, "Why do I want to be married?" and "What do I value most in a potential spouse?"

Some males, or should I call them "dogs," are very skilled at taking advantage of silly women. They are like good actors in a play getting women where they want them psychologically. After many women discover that they've been misused, they complain. They express their disappointment to friends, counselors, mentors, parents and even pastors. Unfortunately, these types of women are blaming men for their own inability to search for what they need. When women focus on fictitious fairy tale fantasies and material desires, it becomes almost impossible to avoid deception. Like most men are ego-driven, women are swayed by their emotions. As a result, flowers, candy, cards, dinners and a few kind words cause selfish women to abort healthy expectations. Our emotions put our bodies into motion. When people control your emotions, they essentially control you. Spontaneity is a good thing, but think first. Fairy tale dreams have caused many women to suffer abuse, infidelity, financial hardship, unplanned pregnancies, sexually transmitted diseases and other misfortunes. Again, "doggish" men are created by silly women. These women are not victims; they are the executive producers of all the drama taking place in their lives.

Avoid relationships that aren't going anywhere. Remember, if you consistently find yourself working on somebody else's character flaws, you are wasting your time! Another benefit of sexual abstinence is getting to know a person and building a friendship without the emotional complications conceived through sex. The initial stages of dating are like a Broadway production with everyone playing a role and an ultimate goal in mind. The intent of dating is to like someone and to be liked in return. The only thing you have to do is sit in the audience, listen, read between the lines and distinguish between "the serious" and "the curious." Some men are looking to fall in love with a virtuous woman. "Doggish" men, on the other hand, sniff their way through unclaimed territory. Like most actors, they reveal their true identity sooner or later. Most often, sexual resistance will expose a person's true intentions. The Bible says "He who finds a wife finds what is good and receives favor from the LORD." *Proverbs 18:22*

The key word in this verse is "finds." This implies that men should make the first approach. The next verse states "and finds favor with the Lord." Men, I hope you understand that God will give you favor when you make a woman your wife. It is very disrespectful for men to play games with women whom they have no intention of marrying.

Women shouldn't seduce or manipulate men into dating or marriage, nor should they send a friend on their behalf to do so. In fact, it's degrading in some cultures for a woman to look at a man enticingly. In America, half-dressed women seduce men every day. Whenever a woman has to chase a man, red flags should go up. The number one reason that most men don't approach women is because they are not interested or not interested enough to approach. Don't waste your time on a man who ignores you. That same lack of initial interest has the potential of reflecting throughout your relationship. Ladies, play it safe and remain virtuous. The search is our responsibility.

Silly, lustful women, who reject wisdom and condone foolishness, encourage bad behavior. They are not widows, or even divorcees, yet they raise children without husbands. They spread diseases. They accept disrespect. They're worse than prostitutes because they give of their bodies freely traveling from one uncommitted man to the next. They're searching for love, but they haven't learned to love themselves. These silly, lustful women create "doggish" men instead of potential, respectful husbands.

Some men don't have a clue on how to treat women. Good examples are limited in broken homes and unhealthy marriages. Most men imitate their fathers, whether good, bad or absent. Unbroken cycles always continue. Trash is intended to be dumped. If you find yourself in a worthless relationship, end it, and destroy all ties. It may seem difficult at first. You might even feel lonely from time to time. You will miss him, but don't call. You might see him, but keep stepping. Emotionally, your heart might hurt for months, even years, but you deserve better. Besides, bad dating relationships make for horrible marriages. Don't destroy your future and then blame your spouse for ruining your life.

18 *While he was saying this, a ruler came and knelt before him and said, "My daughter has just died. But come and put your hand on her, and she will live." 19 Jesus got up and went with him, and so did his disciples.*

20 Just then a woman who had been subject to bleeding for twelve years came up behind him and touched the edge of his cloak. 21 She said to herself, "If I only touch his cloak, I will be healed." 22 Jesus turned and saw her. "Take heart, daughter," he said, "your faith has healed you." And the woman was healed from that moment.

23 When Jesus entered the ruler's house and saw the flute players and the noisy crowd, 24 he said, "Go away. The girl is not dead but asleep." But they laughed at him. 25 After the crowd had been put outside, he went in and took the girl by the hand, and she got up." Matthew 9:18-25

Don't dwell on your past hurts, or present predicaments because we serve a God, who can heal your heart, mind, body, and raise you from any dead situation. If you are hurting because of a past or present situation, I advise you to touch Jesus and allow the healing to begin. Some of your past decisions may be due to your past hurts caused by violence, molestation, emotional abuse, past relationships just to name a few. You are not your actions.

The first step to begin the healing and resurrection process is forgiveness. Forgive yourself for the unwise choices in your past. As soon as you make a choice, it becomes your past. If the choice was unwise and caused you some pain, repent, ask God for forgiveness and forgive yourself. Don't allow guilt to keep you from experiencing new beginnings. The second step is to forgive the person who committed sin against you. I know it's difficult, but we are called by God to forgive. Failure to forgive will keep you in the prison of your past, produce bitterness, gives the devil an open door, and will hinder fellowship with God. You are a child of the King which makes you royalty. If you focus on the main man (Jesus), He will help you choose the right man (husband). Forgive and move on to what God has planned for your life. Allow our Lord and savior Jesus Christ to raise you from that dead place. So learn from your mistakes, and give no man your hand, unless he can lift you up.

Men, who are dogs, may be created by silly women, but a man who finds a wife finds a good thing, and receives favor from the Lord! Rise up mighty woman of God, and help us receive favor from the Lord! We need you! You are bone of our bone and flesh of our flesh, and through you we are delivered into this world. Men and woman were created to dominate the earth together, not to dominate each other.

WORDS OF WISDOM
- Don't chase men, because when you catch him you will continue chasing him to be responsible
- End relationships that are not growing in a positive direction
- Men who are dogs are not born, they are created by silly women
- All men are not dogs, so ask God for wisdom and discernment to help you choose
- Past relationships should teach you what you don't need based on his problems, issues and mistakes
- Past relationships should teach you what you should aspire to become based on your problems, issues and mistakes
- A man who does not know his purpose will waste your time
- God would never take you away from something if he did not have something better to give you
- Being Single is not being "Alone"
- A man will always make time for what is most important to him

CHAPTER THREE

PREGNANT WITH PURPOSE

"My son, do not forget my teaching, but keep my commands in your heart, for they will prolong your life many years and bring you prosperity.

Let love and faithfulness never leave you; bind them around your neck, write them on the tablet of your heart. Then you will win favor and a good name in the sight of God and man.

Trust in the LORD with all your heart and lean not on your own understanding; in all your ways acknowledge him, and he will make your paths straight."

PROVERBS 3:1-6

The following article is an editorial written by a staff member of the Northwest Indiana Post-Tribune. I agree with the problems expressed in the article, but disagree with the editorial solution to a problem that is beyond the boundaries of Gary, Indiana.

I must also acknowledge, and thank the single adults and youth who believe in sexual purity and are living a lifestyle of sexual abstinence. Sexual purity is not impossible, because thousands and perhaps millions are choosing to be sexually abstinent until marriage. They just live by the word of God without the need to express their choice to others. They are what I call the silent majority. When Elijah thought he was the only prophet left in Israel the Lord reminded him, "Yet I reserve seven thousand in Israel-all whose knees have not bowed down to Baal and all whose mouths have not kissed him." *(1 Kings 19:18)*

Sexual purity is about building strong families, and the solution is beyond political parties, race, and what community you live in. Abstinence through sexual purity works! As you read the following article, think about the following questions:

- Am I living a life pleasing to God concerning sexual purity?
- Does my lifestyle set a positive or negative example for youth?
- Am I dating God, but not willing to commit to him through my actions?
- What is the church doing and teaching to assist in eliminating these problems?
- How can I help eliminate this problem?
- Am I a responsible parent?
- Do I talk to my child or children about sex?
- Do we take time and listen to what our youth are trying to tell us

Hey Rudy, some Gary kids could use your help

Northwest Indiana Post-Tribune Editorial
Written by an Editorial Page Editor
October 23, 2009

>   Psst! Rudy! Rudy Clay! Listen up. Set aside all your grand plans for Michael Jackson memorials and downtown renovation and focus on this.
>   You may be about to lose the most valuable agency a city like Gary can have within its borders.
>   And I would suggest you hustle over and do whatever it takes to stop the loss.
>   More than any city in Indiana, Gary needs to have a Planned Parenthood office.
>   Yeah, Rudy, Planned Parenthood is doing more than talking about moving out of the Village Shopping Center.
>   The Planned Parenthood people say the lease there is coming due and they would like to find a less expensive location.
>   I shouldn't have to tell you, Rudy, that one of your city's biggest problems is young, unmarried women — often minors — getting pregnant.
>   It's the babies having babies thing.
>   It's the start of what can be a horrible cycle. A cycle often laced with poverty and crime.
>   A teen without an education likely isn't going to have a job. She can't support a baby, and Lord only knows chances are good the father doesn't have any intention of doing so. It could well be that he is part of the cycle — that he is the son of a woman who got pregnant as a teen and never had a husband.
>   As soon as that teen's baby is born, the two of them become financially dependent on society — particularly Gary, as well as the rest of the taxpayers in Lake County.
>   And the chances are that baby won't stand much of a chance if he or she grows up in poverty, lacking direction. That is especially true if he or she is the first of several children.
>   It is this cycle that is partly responsible for the problems dragging down the Gary school system.
>   We're not talking the Brady Bunch, here, Rudy. We're talking about the potential for a life of drugs, crime and more children born to single mothers.
>   The thing is, Rudy, it doesn't have to be that way.
>   Planned Parenthood is there to help break the cycle.
>   The right-wing religious freaks think Planned Parenthood is nothing but

an abortion mill. Nothing could be further from the truth.

Planned Parenthood, in huge part, is about preventing Unplanned Parenthood.

Just think, Rudy, how much better off your city would be if more sexually active girls were able to walk into Planned Parenthood and get some kind of birth control to help break the cycle.

Don't listen to those do-gooders who preach abstinence. It doesn't work.

The problem is, Rudy, that if Planned Parenthood moves out of Gary, those teens will have a difficult time reaching those who can provide counseling and services.

Planned Parenthood is talking about moving to the west into Griffith at Ridge Road and Broad Street.

You can get to about anywhere in the city of Gary by bus, Rudy, but you can't get to Griffith.

Yet, you may have an ace in the hole over there in Griffith, Rudy. Yeah, can you believe it, Griffith is controlled by Republicans now.

And asking a Republican to embrace a Planned Parenthood office is akin to getting one of them to back a public-option health plan. They know it's good, but they'll never admit it.

It seems that Griffith Town Council President Rick Ryfa didn't like the idea that the clinic can dispense birth control to girls at least 14 years of age.

The Gary clinic, as Griffith would be, is a federal Title X planning agency. And Title X says birth control can be dispensed to those at least 14.

It's important to note, though, that if someone under 14 seeks birth control, Planned Parenthood would be obligated to report it to child welfare officials. There also are reporting requirements for girls 14 and older, depending on the age of their sexual partner.

It's not like a sidewalk sale for condoms.

And, I'm not sure what Ryfa is suggesting.

Maybe 15-year-old girls in Griffith aren't sexually active and thus don't need birth control. Or at least those girls with Republican parents wouldn't think of risking a pregnancy. Yeah, that must be it.

On the other hand, maybe he's suggesting that if a 15-year-old doesn't have access to birth control, she won't become sexually active. Okey dokey.

Maybe he's suggesting that if they bury their heads in the sand that it will all go away.

But chances are that before that ostrich uncorks its head, that 15-year-old will spend prom night changing diapers.

I'm telling you, Rudy, you ought to be thanking your lucky stars that you've got Republicans living next door.

And if I were you, Rudy, I'd be on the horn to Planned Parenthood before those Griffith Republicans wake up and realize that their very own Sarah Palin's daughter could have used the services of Planned Parenthood.

Have you ever wondered why you are still single? Healthy marriages start with passion, preparation and purpose. Do you know God's purpose for your life? There are many more questions you may need to ask yourself, but passion, preparation and purpose are perfect launching pads to success.

DROP IT LIKE IT'S HOT

We are all pregnant with potential, and it is our responsibility to give birth in order to live a fulfilled life. When you make a decision to pursue God's purpose for your life, you will suffer labor pains, but nothing can abort your purpose but you. You are here for a reason. Everyone will go through trials and tribulations. They are inevitable. We will also suffer consequences for the bad choices we make.

Most single people who are having sex are not hoping to produce children. However, unplanned pregnancy or sexually transmitted diseases may very well be the consequences of your actions. Dreams can be destroyed and suffer setbacks, because of unplanned and unwanted pregnancies. It is possible to be a successful single parent, but it will be difficult. Many women I know, who had children during their teenage years or before marriage, wish they would have waited. They expressed how their child or children are a blessing, but the struggles they don't miss.

During my college years, while stomping the yard with my fraternity, I bumped into an old high school fling. She was impressed with my cocky-frat-boy attitude, and I had recently pledged Alpha Phi Alpha. One thing led to another. Not only did we get our grove on, I didn't even use a condom! Hey, it was nothing but a thing for me, just sex. She was not my wife, and I was not interested in marriage at the time. "Darren, I might be pregnant," she said. "What," I replied after hearing her quite clearly! "My period hasn't come yet," she explained. I felt sick and nervous. When I hung up the phone, I felt so stupid. I wondered how would I finish my last year of college and financially take care of the expenses for a newborn with a woman I did not love or want to be with. The next few days I debated joining the military. My future seemed to diminish, and my dreams faded into the dark of night. Days later, she called, "my cycle started!" I silently held the phone, speechless, thankful, relieved, and prepared to give birth to my dreams with a second chance to be responsible. Unfortunately, I had another problem to deal with. She gave me gonorrhea. Still, it could have been worse.

No one usually expects to catch a sexually transmitted disease (STD). One of the biggest problems with STDs is that you can't tell if a person is infected by looking at them. Most people aim to keep it a secret or simply don't know they have one. Every year, three million teenagers are infected with STDs. Sexually active teens and single adults share the same false assumption, "I'm not worried about that, I don't have sex with just anybody, plus I use protection." The only sure way to prevent unwanted pregnancy and sexually transmitted diseases is to practice sexual abstinence. Even the use of a condom is not 100% effective.

There are two types of sexually transmitted diseases, bacterial and viral infections. The STDs that are bacterial or non-viral can be cured with prescribed medication. The most common bacterial STDs are Chlamydia, Syphilis and Gonorrhea according to the Center for Disease and Control. Viral STDs can be treated but not cured. They include Herpes II, Hepatitis B and C, HIV/AIDS and the Human Papillomavirus. It's called "viral" because a living virus is transmitted into your body during your sexual encounter. The human papillomavirus (HPV), a common virus that can be passed from one person to another during sex, is the main cause of cervical cancer and also causes many vaginal and vulvar cancers. It is estimated that of the approximately 6 million new cases of genital HPV in the United States every year, 74% of them occur in 15- to 24-year-olds. That works out to be about 4 million cases a year, or 12,000 a day. To learn more about STDs visit the web site of the Center for Disease Control at www.cdc.gov.

There is a large population of teenagers and adults who think the solution to sexually transmitted diseases and pregnancy is to use a condom. In an effort to combat heightening statistics, Black Entertainment Television (BET) launched a "Wrap it Up" Campaign in which they promoted the use of condoms. I pray that one day BET will also promote the benefits of sexual abstinence. The use of condoms is not a 100% solution to avoid unwanted consequences. Some condoms break, and others get punctured prior to sexual encounters. Many times condoms may come off during intense sex, and various lubricants may not provide effective protection to prevent unwanted pregnancy and diseases. Most of all, my concern is where you are going to spend your eternity when our Lord and Savior Jesus Christ returns?

I remember sitting in the lobby of the Decatur Health Department waiting to see the doctor for STD treatment. The lobby was filled with people of all ages, races and occupations. STDs don't discriminate. First, I was embarrassed to ask my fraternity brother where the health clinic is located. Secondly, I was worried that I might see someone I know while waiting in the lobby. Lastly, as president of my fraternity, I was concerned about my reputation. These were the consequences I faced due to my irresponsible actions that led to me needing treatment for Gonorrhea.

We serve a God who can cure any sexually transmitted disease. I have heard testimonies of how God has cured HIV/AIDS, Herpes, and other viral STDs. Yes, God is a healer, but he wants us to live a Godly lifestyle so we won't be in need of a miracle.

13 The man who was healed had no idea who it was, for Jesus had slipped away into the crowd that was there. 14Later Jesus found him at the temple and said to him, "See, you are well again. Stop sinning or something worse may happen to you." John 5:13-14

EMOTIONAL AND SPIRITUAL CONSEQUENCES

There are many other problems other than pregnancy and STD's that can arise out of pre-marital sex. There are emotional and social issues that usually arise out of being in a sexual relationship. The only condition this web site fails to disclose is the issue of a broken heart when a sexual relationship comes to an end. Have you ever endured a relationship knowing that you were being treated less than a man or degraded as a woman? Perhaps you felt used or rejected after compromising your spiritual beliefs. There are people who experience depression, bitterness, anger, guilt and then question their salvation after engaging in sex before marriage. We have seen or heard numerous stories of how sex and infidelity has destroyed friendships, families, homes, churches, etc. satan is very clever in using these negative behaviors against you to prevent you from doing the work of the Lord. When you fall down, get back up, repent your behavior, and continue to seek the Kingdom of God and his righteousness.

Comprehensive sex education cannot effectively teach prevention of emotional and psychological consequences of sex before marriage. If they taught prevention from this perspective, they would be teaching against themselves. Why? Teaching birth control is promoting sexual activity. Sexual activity outside of marriage is against the word of God. So when you are living in contradiction to the word of God, emotional, psychological, and spiritual problems are going to arise in your relationships. Comprehensive sex education is only concerned with decreasing birth rates, and sexually transmitted diseases. There is no concern for the individuals emotional, psychological, and spiritual state. Sexual activity must stop for the healing to begin from this perspective.

There are several consequences we may face when having a sexual relationship with someone before marriage. Many people tend to think only about the consequences of sexually transmitted diseases and pregnancy. There are also emotional consequences when engaging in sexual relationships outside of marriage. The emotional and spiritual consequences are really the same, and intimacy with God can help you avoid dealing with the spiritual and emotional consequences of sex before marriage. When you allow sin to create emotional instability, you become ineffective for God concerning your contribution to the building of his Kingdom. Emotional and spiritual consequences are outlined below.

FEELINGS OF GUILT AND CONDEMNATION

Sex before marriage is unacceptable for single Christians, and can cause you to become ineffective for the Kingdom of God. Please understand that satan's ultimate goal is to steal, kill and destroy us. When you fall into sin, don't allow guilt to make you ineffective for the Kingdom of God. Feelings of guilt and condemnation will keep you on the sidelines while the battle of bringing in the harvest is being fought. These feelings will make you say things like "When I get my life together I will go back to church" "I need to be free from sin for about three month before I can tell someone about Jesus Christ". We all have fallen short of the glory of God, so repent and rededicate your life to God, and get back on the battle to fight for God.

DAMAGE OF SELF-ESTEEM

Being used for or developing a bad reputation because of sexual activity can cause damage to your self-esteem. This damage is usually multiplied if there is a sexually transmitted disease or an unwanted pregnancy involved. When you use sex to secure a relationship with no success you begin to judge yourself based on another person's perception. You develop your self-esteem by pleasing God. God never changes, so when you look to be pleasing to someone make sure that you are pleasing God in the process.

EMPTINESS AND LONELINESS

Emptiness and loneliness result from the damage of your self-esteem. These two negative emotions will cause you to make quick, unwise decisions in an attempt to fill a void that can only be filled by the love of God. Women must be very careful of these two, because of their need to be loved, have affection and conversation. Be very careful of what man you allow to love you, give you affection, and engage you in conversation.

DOUBTING SALVATION

Don't allow any sin you may fall into cause you to doubt your salvation. The danger of sexual sin is the damage you do to your own body and your intimate relationship with God. satan will sneak in and say "because you did that, God will never forgive you or love you." When you consistently sin, don't repent, and don't live a life pleasing to Him destruction will soon follow. There are a lot of people who sit in church on Sunday who are not saved. There are also people who attend church faithfully, love God and still make mistakes. We are saved by grace and not by works. Please view sexual abstinence as a way to live a life that's pleasing to God, not as a set of difficult rules to follow. I caution you, Christians who live life this way will also be in danger of doubting salvation. Jesus went to the cross to prevent us from living life through the law.

DIMINISHED RELATIONSHIP WITH GOD

When a single person is sexually active, a soul tie develops between the two people involved. Until marriage, we are to have a spiritual and intimate relationship with God. When you are sexually active outside of marriage, your relationship with God becomes distant. You begin to slowly remove God's protection because of your bad choices. You reap what you sow, so be careful what choices you make. Remember there is a difference between consequences of sin and going through trials. God allows trials in your life because he is ready to help take you to the next level. Consequences of sin are a result of your bad choices, and there is no promotion in place after you suffer the consequences. Many people sin consistently, take God's grace for granted and believe that because they attend church on Sunday, they are saved.

1 What shall we say then? Shall we continue in sin, that grace may abound? 2 God forbid! How shall we, that are dead to sin, live any longer therein?
Romans 6:1

FAMILY BREAKDOWN

We have seen or heard of the numerous politicians, actors, musicians, athletes and everyday people who allow sexual immorality to cause major problems for their families. Our single years represent the time to prepare for marriage because marriage will bring its own challenges even for faithful spouses. Our children are hurting and acting out because of bad decisions adults have made.

FACT NOT FICTION

In the 1980s, R&B entertainer Shirley Murdock recorded a song titled "As We Lay." The tune is about an irresponsible couple who engage in an extra-marital affair. One line says, "We forgot about tomorrow as we lay." Still today, many fans sing along with the sinful lyrics. It's unfortunate that this continues to happen in our culture, today. People are having pre-marital affairs and forgetting about the consequences or "tomorrow." Statistics have no musical melody or fancy harmony, but they accurately reflect the reality of our society.

ABSTINENCE IS THE BEST WAY TO AVOID CONSEQUENCES

According to the American Pregnancy Helpline, there are approximately three million unplanned pregnancies in the United States every year.

WHAT ARE SEXUALLY TRANSMITTED DISEASES (STDS)?

STDs are infections or diseases passed from person to person through sexual contact.

HOW MANY PEOPLE HAVE STDS?

The United States has the highest rates of STDs in the industrialized world. In the United States alone, an estimated 15.3 million new cases of STDs are reported each year. Women suffer more frequent and more serious complications from STDs than men.

HOW DO YOU CONTRACT AN STD?

You can contact and spread STDs through kissing, vaginal, anal or oral sex. Some STDs have no symptoms, but can still be passed from person to person.

WHAT'S THE WORST THAT CAN HAPPEN?

AIDS was first identified in the United States in 1981. Since then, the epidemic has been steadily growing. By the end of 2004, there were an estimated 1 million people living with HIV and approximately 415,000 people living with AIDS in the USA. AIDS is also suspected to have killed over half a million Americans. More people become infected every day.

Read and study this book, share it with a friend. There are fatal and frustrating diseases that are infecting our communities. This is a serious concern. Perhaps you're thinking, "I've known him or her for years," and you feel safe having sex with your partner. Remember even married couples undergo unexpected STDs and unplanned pregnancies. As you have read, diseases have spreading throughout our country, and in your neighborhood, partly because of the secrets people don't tell. What is the worst that can happen? The worst thing that can happen for living a life not pleasing to God is to live a life full of conflict, contradiction, confusion, and possibly not inherit the Kingdom of God.

3It is God's will that you should be sanctified: that you should avoid sexual immorality; 4that each of you should learn to control his own body[a] in a way that is holy and honorable, 5not in passionate lust like the heathen, who do not know God; 6and that in this matter no one should wrong his brother or take advantage of him. The Lord will punish men for all such sins, as we have already told you and warned you. 7For God did not call us to be impure, but to live a holy life. 8Therefore, he who rejects this instruction does not reject man but God, who gives you his Holy Spirit. 1 Thessalonians 4:3-8

Nobody is perfect, but you can make the right choices to develop strong positive relationships. This journey begins with an abstinent lifestyle. Great and lasting marriages are inclusive of so much more than sex. If you want to live a quality life, have a healthy and happy marriage and build a beautiful family, its starts with you. Your life is a culmination of the decisions you make. We all have a great destiny awaiting us. The choice is yours.

WORSHIP IN TRUTH

I give hundreds of presentations each year on the benefits of sexual abstinence and how God forgives us for our sins. During my speaking engagements, I provide visual examples of the pitfalls of sex before marriage, benefits of sexual abstinence and the compassion of Christ when we make bad decisions. The following examples will give you an illustration concerning the physical and spiritual benefits of sexual abstinence. As Christians we are called to worship God in Spirit and in Truth, and to use our testimony to bring in the harvest and glorify God.

11But he replied, "The man who made me well said to me, 'Pick up your mat and walk.' "12 So they asked him, "Who is this fellow who told you to pick it up and walk?" 13 The man who was healed had no idea who it was, for Jesus had slipped away into the crowd that was there. 14 Later Jesus found him at the temple and said to him, "See, you are well again. Stop sinning or something worse may happen to you." 15 The man went away and told the Jews that it was Jesus who had made him well. John 5:11-15

EXAMPLE #1: KEEP YOUR CANDY WRAPPED TIGHT

Imagine a lollipop perfectly wrapped and unused. The setting is a church with about 500 people assembled to watch this presentation. "Betty" has the lollipop which represents her virginity. I tell Betty to look out into the audience, and pick out one of the single men and call him up to the stage. Betty picks a young man named "Jeff," and he walks up to the stage. I inform the audience that Betty and Jeff are a couple that has been dating for three weeks, and Jeff is ready to have sex. Betty agrees and gives Jeff her lollipop. This action represents a sexual relationship over a period of time between Betty and Jeff.

For some unspecified reason, the relationship begins to fall apart so Betty asks for her lollipop back. Jeff takes the candy out of his mouth, wraps it up the best way he can and gives the lollipop back to Betty. Since they have broken up, I ask Jeff to stay on the stage but to step aside. I tell Betty to search the audience, and pick another single man and invite him to the stage. You should see the facial expressions of the single men in the audience. They are squirming and hiding to avoid being picked by Betty. Betty picks "Bill," and I motion for him to come on stage with Jeff and me. I explain to the audience that since the breakup, Betty has now started to date Bill. After two weeks of dating, I inform the audience that Bill is ready to have sex with Betty.

I instruct Betty to give Bill her lollipop. Bill looks at me and says "There is no way I am putting that lollipop in my mouth!" The audience roars in laughter at his comment. I then ask Bill why he would not put the lollipop in his mouth that Betty gave him. Bill explains that he saw Jeff had the lollipop in his mouth before him. I ask Bill "If you had not seen Jeff put the lollipop in his mouth before Betty presented it to you, would you have put it in your mouth?" Bill confessed that, in that case, he would have put the lollipop in his mouth.

I raised the lollipop in the air and asked the audience "Is there anyone who would not have put the lollipop in their mouth if you hadn't seen Jeff put the candy in his mouth first?" No one raises their hand. I then ask the audience to focus and take a close look at the lollipop wrapper while posing the question, "Don't you notice that the wrapping paper the lollipop came in has been tampered with?"

Next, I inquired that if I owned a candy store, how many of them would buy anything from me if the wrapping on the candy looked like the wrapping on the lollipop Betty tried to give to Bill. They all laughed, and no one raised a hand. Finally, I asked the audience, "Why is it when someone looks good on the outside, we make a decision to have sex with them without knowing what is on the inside?" Anything can be on the inside waiting for you including pregnancy, soul tie or a sexually transmitted disease(s).

I explained to the audience that this example was used to show how much God loves us in spite of the mistakes we make. All wrappings from lollipops are recycled trash that has been cleaned up for a new day and purpose. We were all recycled trash before we gave our lives to Jesus Christ. Many of us were living a trashy lifestyle, but God picked us up and cleaned us up to be used again for his glory. When you give your life to Christ, you die to old things and become His new creation. Don't unwrap your lollipop until you are married. HEY!!!!

WORSHIP IN SPIRIT
When we live a life pleasing to God, we are worshiping God in spirit and in truth. The first example demonstrated the benefits of living a life of sexual abstinence in the physical. Now, let's take a look at an example of the spiritual.

JOHN 4:7-24
7 When a Samaritan woman came to draw water, Jesus said to her, "Will you give me a drink?" 8 (His disciples had gone into the town to buy food.) 9 The Samaritan woman said to him, "You are a Jew and I am a Samaritan woman. How can you ask me for a drink?" (For Jews do not associate with Samaritans.[a]) 10 Jesus answered her, "If you knew the gift of God and who it is that asks you for a drink, you would have asked him and he would have given you living water." 11 "Sir," the woman said, "You have nothing to draw with and the well is deep. Where can you get this living water? 12 Are you greater than our father Jacob, who gave us the well and drank from it himself, as did also his sons and his flocks and herds?" 13 Jesus answered, "Everyone who drinks this water will be thirsty again, 14 but whoever drinks the water I give him will never thirst. Indeed, the water I give him will become in him a spring of water welling up to eternal life." 15 The woman said to him, "Sir, give me this water so that I won't get thirsty and have to keep coming here to draw water." 16 He told her, "Go, call your husband and come back." 17 "I have no husband," she replied. Jesus said to her, "You are right when you say you have no husband. 18 The fact is, you have had five husbands, and the man you now have is not your husband. What you have just said is quite true."

21 Jesus declared, "Believe me, woman, a time is coming when you will worship the Father neither on this mountain nor in Jerusalem. 22 You Samaritans worship what you do not know; we worship what we do know, for salvation is from the Jews. 23 Yet a time is coming and has now come when the true worshipers will worship the Father in spirit and truth, for they are the kind of worshipers the Father seeks. 24 God is spirit and his worshipers must worship in spirit and in truth."

EXAMPLE #2: THE LIVING WATER
During the next visual example, I use a large glass pitcher filled with water, two glass cups, a can of Pepsi, and a garbage container. I call Betty and Jeff back to the stage along with the pastor of the church. I ask the pastor to hold the pitcher of water. I take the cups and explain to the audience that the cups represent us as two separate but equal temples called "male" and "female" that God created. Betty has one cup and

Jeff has the other. I then ask the pastor to pour water into both cups. This represents God pouring "Spirit Man" into our temples. You know the story. Betty and Jeff begin a sexual relationship outside the will of God. I take the can of Pepsi and pour some of it in the cup (female temple) of Betty and the cup (male temple) of Jeff. If anyone has tasted watered down Pepsi, it not very pleasing to the taste buds. I explain to the audience that the pouring of the Pepsi in the glass cups is the intrusion of sexual sin into the spiritual lives of Betty and Jeff.

Now enters the term "soul tie". A soul tie is a negative spiritual, mental and emotional connection developed from having a sexual relationship with someone to whom you are not married. Have you ever known someone who was in a bad relationship with someone and knew that they needed to end the relationship but just couldn't do it? They would say, "I know I should have been gone a long time ago but I, I just can't let him (or her) go!" That's an example of a soul tie.

Betty and Jeff are now holding their cups (temples) with contamination (Pepsi) in their spirits. After Betty and Jeff break up, they both are having problems in their new relationships because of their past issues. Remember, God is a loving God, and his ways are not our ways. Repenting your sins and turning back to God is the way to clean up your temple.

I ask the pastor to take the full pitcher of water and pour water into the cups of Betty and Jeff until all of the Pepsi has been cleansed from their cups. When you repent your sins, and begin to pray, study, live, meditate on the Word of God and talk to Him, you begin to create an intimate relationship. The water that the pastor poured into the cups represents the living water that Jesus spoke about to the Samaritan woman. Jesus is the living water!

As the pastor continued to pour the fresh water into the glass cups, it started to overflow into the garbage can. The divine purpose of the garbage can is to "catch the mess." When you depend on Jesus as your Lord and Savior, He will absorb all of your mess. Had the garbage can not been there to catch the mess, it would waste all over the place. This is why you can't go to everyone with your problems because they will let "your mess" leak out all over the place. God will never leave nor forsake us. Remember, God is allowing your mess to be recycled. All dirty water goes through a purification process to be used again. To God be the Glory!

Matthew 11:29-30 Take my yoke upon you and learn from me, for I am gentle and humble in heart, and you will find rest for your souls. 30For my yoke is easy and my burden is light."

WORDS OF WISDOM
- A majority of sexually active singles don't expect pregnancy or STD's
- There are some sexually transmitted diseases that are spread through kissing
- The only safe sex is in a marriage where a man and woman are faithful to one another
- Sexually transmitted diseases don't discriminate
- Don't take God's grace for granted by living a sexually immoral lifestyle
- God can cure STDs, but don't test God by having sex before marriage
- There are always consequences to your actions

CHAPTER FOUR

STEPS TO "SAVED" SEX

"So I find this law at work: When I want to do good, evil is right there with me. For in my inner being I delight in God's law; but I see another law at work in the members of my body, waging war against the law of my mind and making me a prisoner of the law of sin at work within my members. What a wretched man I am! Who will rescue me from this body of death? Thanks be to God—through Jesus Christ our Lord!"

ROMANS 7:21-25

TORN

I've got satan to my left
And I've got Gabriel to my right
And they both be whispering in my ear
What Gabriel be saying be coming in kind of fuzzy
But what satan be saying be coming in real clear

I'm Torn
Torn between the sin of Saturday night
And the song of Sunday morn
Between righteousness
And the lustre of brown succulent flesh
Moving languidly in the night
Beconing for me
To come

To come and place my hands upon her mountains
As they erupt
Sending passion and desire
Flowing over the circumference of her being
To dig
Into the dry fertile soil
Of her landscape
And feel
What the new world hath wrought
To become twisted
And entangled
In the tantalizing terror
Of her softness

Dance Salome dance!
And explain to me
Please explain to me
What you will do
With the head of a man

Faithless whore
Temptress of the night
You promise nothing
But death and destruction
Fire and brimstone

Rising to a pinnacle
Twisting and turning
And Burning, and Burning

So what will it be
Heaven's gates
Or Hell's flames
A righteous mans glory
Or a whore's shame

I've got satan to my left
And I've got Gabriel to my right
And they both be whispering in my ear
What Gabriel be saying be coming in kind of fuzzy
But what satan be saying be coming in real clear…

"Psst, Psst, Psst
See that girl in the third pew
She looking at you…
I bet if you sneak her through the back door
You can get her out before anybody know"

I'm haunted
By hellified hips
And halter tops,
Open toe sandals
And daisy dukes,
Dutifully demonstrating
A demonic desire
For lustful liaisons with lips

And she dips
In capri pants
That capriciously captivate my cranium
Causing clandestine kisses and caresses
To cultivate a sinful seed in my spirit

SWEET JESUS

Cut off my hand
Better to lose a hand
Than to burn

Pluck out my eye
Better to lose an eye
Than to face the judgement

See I'm torn
TORN
    TWISTED
        DISTORTED
And I've resorted to…

PRAYER!

Robert L. Jones Jr.

ACCEPT JESUS CHRIST AS YOUR PERSONAL SAVIOR

In order to be successful in living a life of sexual abstinence until marriage, there must be a true spiritual foundation from which to draw. Jesus Christ is the source of my belief and strength. We are saved by grace and not through works, and during difficult times, we must have faith to live a lifestyle of sexual abstinence and purity. Sexual abstinence is a means to an end, which is sexual purity. Be warned that when taking this first step, all Hell will break loose trying to deter you from the commitment you've made.

READ AND STUDY GOD'S WORD

Before beginning the dating process, it's helpful to have a good understanding of God's standards concerning relationships. It will be difficult to choose a spouse if you don't date. The purpose of dating is to build a new friendship with someone of the opposite sex. The problem with dating is that many of these relationships lead to inappropriate behavior. If you quickly become physically and emotionally involved, you are asking for trouble. Reading and studying the word of God will give you the tools necessary to be successful.

I never knew it was wrong to have sex outside of the marriage covenant until I read the Bible. I also found out it was wrong to have sex before marriage from a friend of mine who was sexually active. To live a life pleasing to God, we must read the word of God on a daily basis. The word of God (Bible) is the seed that has the solution to every problem you will face during your lifetime on this earth if you allow it to grow into your soil. If you are a Christian, interested in becoming a Christian or seeking to rededicate your life to Christ, you will never know what is pleasing or detestable to God if you don't read the Word of God.

APPLY GOD'S WORD TO YOUR LIFE

The only way to be successful in living a lifestyle of sexual abstinence is through application of the word of God. This is the most important principle of this book! If you will not apply the Word of God in your life through action, put this book down, and get some sleep! It is important to apply God's Word to our lives daily. It is blessing and our choice to accept Jesus Christ as our Lord and personal savior. We must read and have faith in God's word, because faith without works is dead! If there is no application of what we have read, we will be faced with constant frustration that will weaken your faith in the word of God.

It is not enough to sit in church, receive instruction and then live the same way making the same mistakes. There are many people in relationships that are against the will of God, but they continue to stay in those relationships. There are many people attending church on a weekly basis who are involved in sexual relationships outside of marriage. This is against the Word of God, and don't expect to be blessed if you continue to stay in these relationships. The Word of God is clear in the area of sex, and many individuals wonder why they are having so many problems concerning relationships.

Sex outside of marriage is outside the will of God. Whether you're single, divorced or widowed, the rules are the same for all men and women of God. If you have been sexually active in the past, it will be a challenge to live a sexually abstinent lifestyle. When deciding to live a life pleasing to God, satan will make it difficult. Knowing God's word and not following it shows a lack of faith in God and His word. Church on Sunday should be a Christian Prep Rally to get us focused on living a life pleasing to God, so that He can do great things through us. Most of us feel strong and invincible while in the presence of God while at church hearing His message. The challenge comes when you must apply God's Word to your life and handle the trials that lie ahead.

"Consider it pure joy, my brothers, whenever you face trials of many kinds, because you know that the testing of y our faith develops perseverance. Perseverance must finish its work so that you may be mature and complete, not lacking anything." James 2:4

BE CONTENT IN YOUR SINGLENESS

Many people put on a front when it comes to being content about living single. Many of us look and act content, but inwardly, so many singles feel alone. Do you have friends who are always jumping from relationship to relationship? Do you have friends who come to you for council concerning their relationships? Have you ever given a friend good advice about a relationship, only to be ignored? No one is perfect, because we've all fallen short, but we must practice being content with ourselves and the love of Jesus.

Truthfully speaking, many of us are not ready for a spouse. It's interesting, because I've met so many married people who want to be single and countless singles who want to be married. I've been told by many of my happily married friends, "Wait on God's timing when choosing your wife."

Choosing a wife or accepting a husband is an important decision. It should be made with careful consideration and amongst good council. Living single affords individuals an opportunity to fulfill their life's purposes without distractions. If you are single, it is for a reason. Are your finances in order? Do you have a job? How is your credit? Are you fulfilling God's purpose in your life? Are you mature enough to be married? How much debt do you have? Do you have an intimate relationship with God? Do you have integrity? Can you be faithful in a relationship? Do you have anger issues? Do you attend church on a consistent basis? Do you tithe? It is not a mistake as to why you are single, so at this time renew your mind and focus on areas in need of improvement so when your husband or wife is revealed, you will be ready.

Most important, learn to love yourself, rid your life of discontentment, and live without regrets. This journey begins with abstinence and learning to be happy with self. Do not look for someone to complete you. That's not being selfish. It's learning to love the person living inside. Living single should bring as much joy as marriage.

YOU MUST DEVELOP A DESIRE FOR SEXUAL PURITY

In order to be successful with sexual abstinence until marriage, you must passionately want to live a life of sexual abstinence. When you make the decision to be sexually pure, attacks will come from everywhere to distract your focus. You will not be successful if you revert to giving in to the same thoughts that encouraged your previous sexual activity. This is clearly not a lifestyle for weak-minded individuals. The art of abstinence requires a "by any means necessary" approach. It has to mean as much as life and death. You must get a firm grip on this belief, and live it without compromise or shame.

KEEP COMPANY WITH SUPPORTIVE PEOPLE

The people you allow to occupy space in the auditorium of your mind will play a major role in your life. No one can force friendships on you or excommunicate family members for you, but these individuals play an important part in your growth and development. If you have friends who are not helping you grow and develop from their interaction, search for new friends. If you have friends who are not supportive of your commitment to sexual abstinence, cut them loose. If you have friends who encourage you to be sexually active before marriage, kick them to the curb. Surround yourself with men and women who will give you Godly council when times get rough. We need friends who are supportive and will help keep us focused on our goals.

KEEP YOUR EMOTIONS IN CHECK

Don't allow your emotions to take over because they will control your actions. At any given time your emotions can change. If you are not careful, emotions can get you trapped in troublesome situations. Think with your mind instead of reacting to your emotions. Have you ever met someone so attractive that you made an unwise decision? Think about a relationship that ended when the person you were dating showed their real colors.

After everything is said and done, some people are not everything they portray themselves to be. How often do you hear of relationships unexpectedly ending in heartache, pain, loneliness, resentment, unwanted pregnancies, credit card debt, sexually transmitted diseases, broken hearts, and other problems? Emotions are designed to help us celebrate, empathize, sympathize, understand and relate to others, but many people never let others know the truth about how they feel. When this happens, innocent people are left miserable with regrets and disappointments.

Loneliness is a major problem for many women concerning the need to engage in sexual activity before marriage. This negative emotion (Root) can cause problems for women because their needs are love, affection and conversation. As singles we must understand the difference in being alone and being lonely.

PUT YOUR EYES ON A DIET

One of the top three needs for men is sex, so while living a life pleasing to God; a line must be drawn between what is decent and what is indecent. Think about the sexually seductive images displayed on television and movie screens. They cause you to meditate on the very lifestyle you're trying to avoid. Even worse, watching pornography is the primary root of masturbation which is idol worship. These additions have risen to mountain levels destroying intimacy, marriages, self image, families, and distorting how men and women view each other. Visual stimulation is a major problem when it comes to sex. This is where most men fall off the bandwagon. Any man who disagrees with this notion is lying to himself, unless he's blind, deaf, or dumb.

We have a responsibility to monitor what we view and what we allow our minds to process.

3 For though we live in the world, we do not wage war as the world does. 4 The weapons we fight with are not the weapons of the world. On the contrary, they have divine power to demolish strongholds. 5 We demolish arguments and every pretension that sets itself up against the knowledge of God and we take captive every thought to make it obedient to Christ. 2 Corinthians 10:3-5

Beauty is in the eye of the beholder. What is unattractive to one person may be beautiful to another. What does this have to do with sexual abstinence? We live in a society that dictates how we should look, dress and act. We look at commercials, read books and watch videos on how to lose weight and look better. Healthy eating and daily exercise is important to the human body, but beauty is something that should come from within.

Here's why we must be careful. What you spend your time viewing can cause lustful emotions to appear in your heart. Think for one moment about all the movies and television programs that highlight sex appeal and sexual relationships. If you are not careful, you may begin to accept these visuals as normal, and then believe that sex outside of marriage is okay. Sexually active people say "As long as you are honest and up front, it's okay," or "But we love each other," or "We use protection," or "That's the only person I'm with." These are in part products of media influenced relationships.

If you are not careful of what you watch, a door will open, which can cause you to do what you usually consider unthinkable. Even worse, it can influence you to stay in the same situation you've been in for years. This is most important for men because for centuries, we have looked at women as objects of desire instead of God's creation to be loved and respected. As men we must learn how to starve our eyes. We must be very careful of how long we look because a look can become a fixation, and a fixation is bound to become lust. I know that women also lust, but it is more of a problem for men because one of the top primary needs for men is sex. The root for sexual immorality in men is caused by lust.

There is nothing wrong or immoral about noticing or even acknowledging attractive people. The problem presents itself when a look turns into lust. Lust normally begins with a quick glance that evolves into a continued stare. It's almost as if you're trying to take a mental snapshot to view at your convenience. Never stare. It's a general consensus that people think it's rude and makes most people uncomfortable.

It is okay to appreciate beauty, but don't allow beauty to ruin your focus. Don't allow what you see to overshadow your beliefs. There are some women who take matters into their own hands. Remember, "When a man finds a wife, he finds a good thing." There are ways to make your presence known without chasing men because the man you are chasing probably is not looking for you anyway.

Don't allow your admiration to elevate someone to idol status because you are headed for trouble. When you idolize a person, you aim to please people, not God. This is the worst scenario to enter when trying to live sexually abstinent because manipulators take advantage of "people pleasers." Be careful when you claim a husband or wife in the name of Jesus and elevate that person to idol status. If things don't work out the way you planned, don't blame God; blame yourself. Everything you chase is not worth catching, and everyone searching is not worthy of your time. Sometimes, eye-catching men and women are not worth a second glance. Keep your eyes on the prize because your ultimate reward is living a life that is spiritually, emotionally and physically healthy.

WATCH WHAT YOU WEAR

Men and women must be mindful of the type of clothing we wear. Some types of clothing make certain people look like they are advertising themselves and soliciting sex. While the saying goes, "Never judge a book by its cover," most marketing strategists develop book covers, television commercials and magazines to sell products. Tight clothing, short skirts, skimpy tank tops, revealing cleavage, seductive make-up and flashy jewelry often define sex appeal in our culture. Sexy music videos, sexual subliminal content in television sitcoms and terms like "hot," "fine" and "sexy" all suggest that sex is the ultimate goal.

Men are often stimulated visually. For some, how a woman looks is a top priority when choosing a potential mate. Many women sell themselves short by wearing unacceptable clothing to attract men. I know many men and women keep their bodies in great physical condition, and some are blessed with a naturally beautiful physical appearance. Unfortunately, some women garner the wrong attention and often receive unwanted gestures and comments. Ideally, everyone should be able to wear anything they want, but that's not the case in our society, especially if you expect respect.

Respect is important. We don't live our lives based on other people's opinion of us, but other perspectives are meaningful. Women who wear revealing clothing should not get angry when they get unwanted attention. Why would you get angry when you wore that seductive clothing motivated by the desire to get attention? If you want to attract bears, put on honey and go into the woods.

People who are sure of themselves get attention based on their intelligence and confidence. Their presence alone demands respect. Sex appeal, on the other hand, can be a form of manipulation. If you plan to practice prevention and avoid pre-marital sex, you won't be able to pattern your life after some movie stars, rap artists and other celebrities who capture the limelight. Make a difference by starting with the first impression you make on others. This impression is often non-verbal and usually based on your attire and physical attributes. You can look stunning without giving in to sexual desires, and feel beautiful without ending up on your back in the bedroom.

NO COMPANY AT HOME ALONE

Living a lifestyle of sexual purity is about prevention not reaction. This is why you should always have an informal chaperone present during intimate settings. I know many of you feel old enough and mature enough to have a man or woman alone in your home, but think "prevention!" If you want to spend alone time with that special person, do so in public places. Otherwise, you should hang out with a group of friends. There's safety in numbers! Most adults will admit that pre-marital sex often happens spontaneously. This is one of the most ignored warnings concerning sexual abstinence, and many people live life with regret as a result. Many of us can recall a time when we felt that we were strong enough to handle a situation, and a few hours later we wondered "How did I let that happen?" The further you walk away from the edge, the safer your journey will be to a promising future.

BE CLEAR, UNCOMPROMISING AND CONSISTENT

Make it clear to the person whom you are dating that you want to live a sexually abstinent lifestyle until marriage. If you are honest in the beginning, the tone is set.

When you begin dating someone, it is obvious that there is an attraction so be careful. It's easy to be sexually abstinent with someone you only view as a friend, or do not have a physical attraction to. When you meet a person you have a strong attraction for and appears to be the "complete package," be careful! Never compromise your beliefs in order to make a person stay in the relationship.

When dating, make sure that he or she is supportive of your commitment to sexual purity. Regardless of their attractiveness or wealth, if the person is not respectful of your commitment, you don't need them. In the beginning, make your convictions on this issue clear. Stick to what you know is right, and you will begin to see if he or she is an asset or liability. We must also remain consistent on our path to sexual purity. Don't talk and preach sexual purity for three months and have sex with that person, then go another four months and have sex again. There are some people you can win over to Christ because of your stand on sexual purity. Many singles are caught in a serious struggle of trying to live their life pleasing to God. In the beginning of a dating relationship you will not know their sexual past, but staying true to the word of God can show them that it is possible to be sexually pure.

FOCUS ON FRIENDSHIP

It is easy being friends with someone to whom you are not attracted. Difficulties and challenges arise when you meet an attractive person who makes your heart skip beats. The concept of delayed gratification is a serious problem concerning aspects of everyday life for some people. People seek anything that gives quick or temporary gratification, from money and food to sexual pleasures.

When people learn to focus on lasting friendships, it enables healthy relationships to form. I know I'm not the only person who has rushed into a relationship. Afterwards, I felt stupid for allowing my emotions to take control. If you always focus on building better friendships, it becomes easier to relate, wait and maintain innocent and honest boundaries.

Building friendships prevent people from polluting pure relationships with lust and idol worship. When these types of friendships flourish into marriage, they launch from a foundation built on concrete, not sand. If the friendship doesn't flourish into marriage not crossing certain boundaries can help in maintaining a distant friendship and a certain amount of respect for that person.

AVOID INTIMATE KISSES

Kissing arouses emotions that can cause relationships to automatically move to the next level. No, sex will not always result from kissing, however, emotional ties often develop, and broken hearts occur all too often. For some people, kissing is as common as shaking hands. To others, it is sacred. Nonetheless, kissing is an intimate expression of various emotions. Ladies, you need to be very careful when it comes to kissing. For most, a kiss is a gentle and innocent expression of love. For most men, kissing appeases the ego by marking unclaimed territory.

Until you have a marital commitment, perhaps it is best to avoid such advances. Remember, men and women in most cases view kissing differently. A simple kiss may not lead couples into the bedroom, but it can possibly result in a broken heart leading to conflict, contradiction and confusion. Remember that if you are lusting and lonely, kissing can become the gateway that can lead you to sexual activity, and an emotional connection that may be difficult to break. Always check yourself before things get to hot to handle.

NO SLEEPOVERS

Sleeping in the same bed with someone you are not married to, or allowing them to stay the night in your home is walking on dangerous ground. Can a barefoot person walk across hot coals and not be burned? If you can sleep in the same bed and have sex on occasion, you can get married. If you lose track of time during a date, and you fail to get a chaperone, go to your individual homes. I don't care if the person is sleeping in the guest room. There may be too much temptation to tip toe into the other person room. Don't sleep over, even if your intentions are pure. The atmosphere is almost guaranteed to change when you're half-awake, music softly playing, and the sensation of a warm body cuddled next to your half-dressed, warm-blooded flesh. Sleeping in the same bed before marriage is almost like begging for sex without actually verbalizing it. When you are in a relationship (committed or not) and are physically/emotionally attracted to that person, sleeping in the same bed is not a wise thing to do.

NO ORAL SEX

If you are serious about trying to live a lifestyle of sexual purity, oral sex cannot be an option. There are many people in our society who feel that oral sex is okay because it is not penetration. Oral sex is not an acceptable alternate to pre-marital sex.

In the heat of the moment, people stop thinking and start reacting based on their emotions. So, think ahead. Oral sex poses the risk of contracting a sexually transmitted disease. In addition, there are emotional, psychological, and spiritual consequences that will follow as well.

Ideally, most people would not want to marry a person with a reputation of performing oral pleasures with multiple past partners. Although pregnancy is avoided through oral sex, without marriage, it is irresponsible and degrading as it relates to your future spouse. You cannot be sexually immoral and have an intimate relationship with God.

PURSUE YOUR DREAMS WITH ANOINTING AND POWER

Getting involved with various activities of interest and setting life goals can assist you in living a lifestyle of sexual abstinence. At the end of each day, I am so tired until my focus is on going to sleep. Regardless of how tired a person may be, you can still find trouble. Working, pursuing your dreams, and achieving your goals help keep the mind occupied and your life fulfilled. My focus is allowing God's will to be done in my life. Every day, I ask God to give me favor in everything that I do for the advancement of his Kingdom. Keep striving, pushing, and moving no matter what your circumstances are.

I understand bills need to be paid, business must be taken care of, and other priorities need attention. I encourage you to stay focused but attentive, because an opportune time for the enemy is when we are emotionally, mentally, and physically drained. Working a lot of hours, emotional stress, and lack of sleep can make it extremely difficult to stand against temptation. Abstinence is about prevention, and if you are serious about winning this battle, you must be active and focused.

LISTEN TO THE HOLY SPIRIT AND OBEY

There are three voices we hear — God's, our own, and satan. The Holy Spirit will never guide you in the wrong direction. The problem is that many of us know when God is telling us not to get involved in unholy relationships, but we do it anyway. We feel that we are strong enough to handle a situation and think that if things get difficult, we will be strong enough to make the correct choice. Many of us are faced with difficult decisions to make on a daily basis. The greatest gift we have been given by God outside of Jesus Christ is the ability to make choices through our own free will. God and satan can have strong influence in our lives, but we are responsible for the choices that we make. Listen when the Holy Spirit says that going to a woman or man's home at 2:00a.m.is not a wise idea.

"So, if you think you are standing firm, be careful that you don't fall! No temptation has seized you except what is common to man. And God is faithful; he will not let you be tempted beyond what you can bear. But when you are tempted, he will also provide a way out so that you can stand up under it." 1 Corinthians 10:12-13

DON'T FIGHT WHEN YOU CAN RUN!!!!

If you ever find yourself in a situation where things are getting hot and heavy too fast, get out as soon as you can! Always think "prevention," and don't allow yourself to get into a position where it may be too difficult to resist temptation. It is easy to say what you would do if you found yourself in a certain situation, but to stand firm or flee when temptation visits takes faith. We must be strong and make the correct choice.

One evening while sitting on the living room couch at the home of an extremely beautiful woman, an inner voice conversation began. We had just gone to dinner and were talking and watching television. She put her arms around me, kissed me on the cheek, laid her head on my shoulder and thanked me for dinner. I began to hear two voices in my head speaking on what my next move should be. One voice was telling me to take advantage of the moment by getting this woman into the bedroom, taking her clothes off and taking care of business. I knew this was the voice of satan because having sex before marriage is sin and not God's will for my life.

The other voice was telling me that it was time to go home and get some sleep because I had placed myself in a position that had potential to get out of control. I knew this was the voice of God.

The third voice told me to stay for a few more hours because I was strong enough to say "no" if the situation escalated. I knew this was my own voice because I was trying to figure out a way to stay and not cross the line. This is where many of us make the terrible mistake of thinking we can handle everything on our own. After remembering my commitment to sexual purity, I informed the young lady it was time for me to go home. The most important point from this example is that I should have listened to the Holy Spirit when it told me to go home after dinner. It was stupid to put myself in such a situation.

As Christians, we must make choices that will not put us in situations where sin may be too great to resist. Many of us do not understand the power of temptation until after the sin has been committed and we are begging the Lord for forgiveness. God loves us so much that He will always present a way to escape sinful opportunities. It felt refreshing to know that I was able to refocus my attention and not cause any harm to that young lady or myself. This was also a battle with temptation that I could have avoided from the beginning. Some of our unnecessary fights can be avoided by not getting into the boxing ring.

LIVE SEXUAL ABSTINENCE ONE DAY AT A TIME

The commitment of living a lifestyle of sexual abstinence until marriage is challenging. We live in a society that approves, supports and advocates pre-marital sex. The best way to abstain until marriage is to commit on a daily basis. Most New Year's resolutions fail within the first few weeks or months because we place emphasis on the entire 365 days.

DEAL WITH TODAY

Every morning after I read some scripture, I make a pledge to God to remain sexually abstinent until marriage for that day by reading the pledge card that I signed. Each morning, make the commitment to God and yourself that today you are going to be sexually pure.

THINGS TO REMEMBER
STEPS TO SAVED SEX

1. Accept Jesus Christ as your personal savior
2. Read and study God's Word
3. Apply God's word to your life
4. Be content in your singleness
5. Develop a desire for sexual purity
6. Keep company with supportive people
7. Keep your emotions in check
8. Put your eyes on a diet
9. Watch what you wear
10. No company at home alone
11. Be clear, uncompromising, and consistent
12. Focus on friendships
13. Avoid intimate kisses
14. No sleepovers
15. No oral sex
16. Pursue your dreams with anointing and power
17. Listen to the Holy Spirit and obey
18. Don't fight when you can run
19. Live sexual abstinence one day at a time
20. Deal with today

CHAPTER FIVE

HONESTY IS THE BEST POLICY

"Do not be yoked together with unbelievers. For what do righteousness and wickedness have in common? Or what fellowship can light have with darkness? 15 What harmony is there between Christ and Belial? What does a believer have in common with an unbeliever?"

CORINTHIANS 6: 14-15

While living single, it is our responsibility to avoid activities that may possibly lead to sex. For those who are married, it is your responsibility to limit sex to your spouse. No matter what motivates you to practice an abstinent lifestyle, nothing will remove your sexual urges. We are humans, regardless of our religious confession, spiritual beliefs or personal commitments. Sexual desire will always be a reality for a majority of people. How you respond to this reality can determine your destiny. Sex is a legitimate need, and God blessed marriage as the only way to fill this legitimate need.

No man or woman has the power to control you unless you allow them. No one can make you have a sexual relationship. Depending on your desires, others can have a strong influence, but not total control. If a sexual relationship exists, it is because you wanted it to happen. Perhaps if I say that you "gave in to temptation," it sounds better. We can't afford to let our flesh control our actions. Sexual abstinence enables people to take control of their desires before making life-long commitments.

In any opposite-sex friendships, we must be very careful not to send mixed signals. In most opposite-sex friendships involving singles, someone in that relationship may have more of an attraction to a person than that person has to them. If both friends are mature, and boundaries are not crossed, the friendship can be a blessing. It is easy to possess a pure friendship with someone to whom you are not physically attracted. Unfortunately, men have more difficulties dealing with and resisting physical attractions. Its best that men remove themselves from sexual temptations, otherwise, they will surrender to sexual perversions. I am specifically speaking of the men who entertain the "friends with benefits" philosophy.

If you detect a sudden change in a friend's attitude, and sense that he or she is gaining an interest that may or may not be welcomed, be careful. If you do, or don't share the same or similar interest, be open and honest and leave no room for assumption. It's your responsibility to keep relationships in perspective and respectful by creating boundaries so there is no room for miscommunication. This is a sure remedy to eliminate secret desires from raging out of control. In order to avoid unwanted problems, always use good discretion.

It is understood that in order to find your wife, there must be a search. This is where dating comes in. Although dating can get complicated, it's also important. It helps people discover the true character of others. Dating is the only way to search the hearts of people we have an interest in marrying. In today's society, dating must be approached seriously. So many people have hidden agendas and untold secrets that could ruin a marriage if discovered too late.

Women must also be sure to take notice of malicious male motives. It's no secret that some men date or pursue women for reasons other than marriage. These self-centered men want sex, maids, cooks and cover-ups. Men must also be on the lookout. There are also women who pursue or date men for reasons other than marriage. First, be aware of needy women who pursue men. Often, they are looking for someone to fill a void. Instead of looking at how to solve their own problems, they go from man to man looking for a savior. When they find out that a man cannot solve their problems, they use him as a scapegoat by blaming him for all of their problems. Remember, honesty is the best policy. Many men fall into this trap because they want women to be dependent on them. Most men will try to play the role of savior, especially if sex is in the formula. When the sex gets old, and needs becomes nerve-wrecking, the man tries to bounce. He then finds out that this woman has become an emotional resentful "fatal-attraction" type whom he will have difficulty avoiding. Also, be aware of people who pursue or date you because of your material blessings.

DATING WITHOUT DIPPING

The purpose of dating is to assist you in building friendships to help you choose the correct mate for marriage. We really should not date until we are satisfied with being alone and not lonely. Many older singles put an age or time limit on marriage which is the wrong thing to do. We tell God "If you don't hurry up and send me my spouse, I will find him or her on my own!" The first mistake is to think that God will tell you who to select as your spouse. Many people want to put this major responsibility on God, but that is not how He works. God will never choose our spouse for us because we have free will to make choices. God doesn't even make us become Christians. He gives us free will to live righteous or unrighteous.

As Christians, we have the word of God to help us in our search by reading, studying and living by the word of God. God will provide us with opportunities to meet people, but will never choose for us. Some people spend a lot of time waiting on God to send that special someone. Be careful, because when you wait (which is a waste of time) you begin to get frustrated and lower your standards because you feel God is taking too long. You then get desperate and hook up with the first person that you find reasonable. Understand satan can also place counterfeit people in your path to assist you in making unwise choices. Knowing that we have free will to make choices, we must study and live by Christian kingdom principals. Understanding these principals with prayer will help you develop the ability to choose wisely during difficult moments.

Blessings also come through people, so become a productive man or woman of God, and don't expect your spouse to fall from the sky.

Many men and women have been used and abused for their wealth and material possessions. These people become bitter, hateful and give negative labels to all members of the opposite sex such as, "All men are dogs," or "All women are gold diggers." These people are really embarrassed and resentful because of the warning signs that they ignored in the beginning of the relationship. When you begin to date someone, don't allow bad character to corrupt good company. Regardless of how attractive or wealthy someone is, listen to the Holy Spirit when he tells you it's time to cut that person loose. Often, we have a false sense of perception of thinking we can change someone, when we are only responsible for ourselves.

When a man clearly knows a woman could never be his wife, he should let her go so she can be blessed by another mighty man of God! Ladies, if you don't feel like the relationship is advancing, let him go so you won't become bitter and make the next man pay for your past mistakes! Never try and convince someone to be or stay in a relationship if they don't want to be there. Never add insult to injury. In this case, don't add sex to a stagnant relationship and start pulling tricks to get a commitment. The truth might hurt, but it always sets you free. If a man hasn't discussed marriage within the first year of your relationship, then he may be dealing with some internal issues that may not have anything to do with you. Perhaps he has a fear of commitment. Maybe there's something about you that he just can't accept. He could be a brother on the down low, dating someone else on the side, man or woman. Whether it's a year, 52-weeks or 365 days, however you phrase it, it is more than enough time to discover your wife. Men, be honest. A woman may not like your honesty, but in the end, you will gain her respect for being truthful.

Actions will always speak louder than words. Either you're ready or you're not. Stop wasting time. You might have him or her fooled, because it's easy for women to get hooked on a fairy tale fantasy or for men to want the perfect woman. My goal is to expose your games, tell the truth, and pray that wisdom follows. Your problem starts with the man in the mirror. Mature adults understand that honesty is the best policy followed by making Godly choices.

Learning to control your flesh starts with controlling your thoughts. People feel bound to submit to their own way of thinking, but thoughts can be elevated. If you can change the way you think, then you'll change the things you do. If you change the things you do, you will change the way you live. Men and women should not misuse one another for selfish desires. I don't care if you are honest about what you want. Honesty means nothing if you still make a foolish choice. Let's be more specific. When you feel lonely, don't fill that time with dating. Unfortunately, and most often, women think you're grasping for a more intimate relationship. In reality, you were just filling a void of boredom.

As difficult as it is to admit it, some men date women just to kill time. These men are secretly waiting for a better package to present itself. Men, married and single, often say, "There's nothing wrong with just looking." Never forget that when lust takes control, a quick glance will ruin your ability to make sound decisions. Gain control of your flesh and eyes. Ladies, when a man chooses not to spend time with you because "he's just not that in to you," don't get mad. Be grateful that he has taken your feelings in consideration. When making choices concerning relationships, some women think that men are insensitive creatures who are inconsiderate of their feelings.

Choosing a spouse will be one of the most important life-altering decisions ever. If you're not careful, divorce will be another life-altering decision. Don't let the physical appearance of a woman or a man's finances become the only ingredient you use when choosing a potential spouse. Some men often use sweet phrases to get what their eyes are attracted to. Some women use a beautiful body and a pretty smile to get what they want, and neither is enough to make a marriage last.

People have a moral responsibility to treat one another with respect. Respect and honesty work hand in hand. Honesty followed with Godly choices is always the best policy.

DIVINE DATING FOR DUMMIES

There is no need to speak to you about sexual abstinence if there is no wisdom or discernment about dating. The majority of sinful sexual behavior takes place during the dating phase while singles are getting to know one another. This behavior will cause the persons involved problems when it's time to complete their evaluation of one another. Building a new friendship without extreme emotional, spiritual and physical attachment will allow wisdom and discernment to take their rightful place during the evaluation process. The following guidelines will help you when you need to make the decision whether to: (1.) continue the relationship with the belief that marriage can become a reality, (2.) become friends only, (3.)realize that a distant or casual friendship wouldn't be a wise choice for one or both of you (4.) or walk away, and never look back.

TAKE YOUR TIME

During the dating process, please take it slow and don't rush. Take time to get to know the person because there is a lot that you don't know. You will not be able to fully know someone during a short period of time. It's silly to think that you will get to know all the positives and negatives in a three to six-month period. Taking your time will prevent you from getting emotional too quickly. I know it's challenging to keep your cool when you meet someone who can influence your heart to beat extremely fast. Remember, emotions change so take it slow. Also, it's not necessary to see that person every day of the week. Leaving sex out of the picture will allow you to not get attached to someone you barely know. Taking your time will allow you to break free from a relationship with a minimum amount of spiritual and emotional time spent on the wrong person.

BE STRATEGIC

During this time of building your new friendship, be strategic in your actions. Use your wisdom and knowledge of the Word because your heart has the ability to deceive. Start off with telephone conversations to allow your ears to hear what that person is saying. When led by the spirit of God, I don't care how attractive someone is, you are able to actually listen when they're talking. After hearing what they say, you may get a revelation to not pursue (men) or go out on a date (women). When getting to know someone, there is no need to give up too much information. There is no need to provide all of your private information to someone. You don't know if this person is going to be your spouse. If you give up certain information too soon, it may scare your date away. You also don't want your personal and private information the talk of the town or church either!

STAY CONNECTED TO GOD

Some single Christians are praying for God to send them a spouse. What's interesting is that when they start to date someone, God is placed on a shelf or counter only to be studied, worshiped and praised when they need something. Staying connected to the Word of God is important. During the dating process, following the Word of God is key. Like emotions, people change, but God never changes! It would be ignorant to think that singles will not hold hands, hug and kiss in relationships. At the very least, (permitted by the couple) these actions should only take place within a committed, monogamous relationship. These actions should never be the means to gaining a committed relationship. I also caution, as I did earlier, to be careful concerning intimate kissing. Is kissing and hugging a sin? No, but lust is sin. So be very careful that your actions don't lead to sexual immorality. Staying connected to God will help you focus while dating or engaging in committed, monogamous relationships.

FELLOWSHIP WITH FRIENDS AND FAMILY

It is critical to stay connected to friends and family. These are the people who should always have our back. Through our own experiences and interactions with people, we should have an idea of who our real friends are. There is a clear difference between friends and acquaintances. Friends are people you can count on in the good times and bad. Acquaintances are only there to see how they can benefit by connecting themselves to you. If they can get to their goal quicker through another person, they will drop you like a hot coal. Most acquaintances are not bad people. You simply need to know the difference to avoid bitterness when they reveal who they really are. Our friends, to a certain extent, should be involved in our dating lives. We must use Godly wisdom and discernment in choosing our friends as we would our future spouse. Godly friends can see things you may not be able to see and will be able to provide council from a different perspective. Your immediate family may play a major role in choosing a spouse. If your dating relationships get to this stage, it's always good to listen to the advice of parents, siblings and other trustworthy family members. Remember, in the end, the decision is yours.

LOVE TKO

In the early 1980's, legendary soul singer Teddy Pendergrass had a hit called "Love TKO," a boxing term which means "technical knockout." The song is about a man who is in a relationship with a woman, and he is giving her all his time, love, sex and money. None of these actions or things is helping him to win the love of this woman. One famous lyric from this song says, "It's time to let it go, looks like another love TKO." I know it's difficult to leave a relationship that you want to work so badly. When sex is involved and soul ties develop, this makes the breakup all the more difficult when you get a revelation to let that person go. Here are some of the reasons why a relationship must end or never begin:

NO SPIRITUAL COMPATIBILITY

It is amazing that many Christian singles don't have a personal relationship with our Lord and Savior Jesus Christ. You can't get into a relationship with someone who is spiritually ignorant with the thought that you can save them. Don't allow the enticement of physical and material things to compromise your Christianity. In trying to change someone, you may ultimately be the person who changes.

NO GODLY CHARACTER OR INTEGRITY

If you are dating or in a relationship with someone who is mean, dishonest, unfaithful, mentally unstable, disrespectful, selfish and lazy, let them go! You don't need to hear a voice from heaven to help you make the obvious decision. If you are reading, and studying the Word of God, this is a no-brainer.

NO ROMANTIC OR PHYSICAL ATTRACTION

If you are not attracted to the person you are dating, this is a sign. Dating someone you have no attraction to is dangerous, and it is unfair to the person you are dating. Don't continue this relationship hoping things will change because you are enjoying other benefits. Don't play games! If there is no attraction, be honest with yourself and say "no" to the dinners, money and gifts. Stop sticking around until a bigger and better deal presents itself. When you have a relationship with God, being single is not being lonely.

EMOTIONAL AND PHYSICAL ABUSE

If someone is putting their hands on you, calling you out of your name and/or being emotionally abusive, it's time to bounce. This person not only needs Jesus, but they need counseling, and you can't give it to them. Cut them loose!

CONSTANT FIGHTING

If there are more arguments than there are moments to help strengthen your friendship, let it go. Consistent arguing is a foundation for future emotional and physical abuse.

OUTSIDE OF GOD, YOU ARE NOT A PRIORITY

All people make time for what is most important to them. If you are not a top priority, take this into strong consideration. If they won't make you priority now, will they during your marriage? If you are not a priority, a sexual relationship won't change the priority list. You will only become a priority when they want to have sex.

CHAPTER SIX

SEX AND THE CHURCH

"Those whom I love I rebuke and discipline. So be earnest, and repent. Here I am! I stand at the door and knock. If anyone hears my voice and opens the door, I will come in and eat with him, and he with me. To him who overcomes, I will give the right to sit with me on my throne, just as I overcame and sat down with my Father on his throne. He who has an ear, let him hear what the Spirit says to the churches."

REVELATION 3: 19-20

WHAT MUST THE CHURCH DO?

The church is responsible for creating a loving atmosphere where people are welcome to enter God's temple to hear the uncompromising word of God. Pastors are responsible for teaching the entire word of God, no matter how uncomfortable it may be to the membership or visitors. All have sinned and fallen short of the glory of God. If you keep on living, you are going to make mistakes. People attend church for various reasons. Most people become Christians and join church to become better people, gain a better understanding of the word of God and lead others to Jesus Christ. Some people join a church to network; find a spouse, increase popularity, or use grace as a license to sin.

As Christians, we have an obligation to go out and make disciples of all nations. As members of the congregation, we must not put all of the responsibility on church leadership to assist us in living a life pleasing to the Lord. Pastors cannot be responsible for their members reading, studying and meditating on the word of God. Your pastor cannot make you create an intimate relationship with God. That is your responsibility. The pastor is responsible for teaching the Word of God to the church membership in a method in which they can understand. The pastor is also required to live by the word of God that he or she is preaching and teaching.

During these tough economic times, and for the rest of your life you will be tested. No one said that when you became a Christian life would be easy. There are going to be times of testing in your life. Stay strong and focused. There will be times in your life where there will be no promotion without prosecution, no triumph without testing, and no success without storms. We must go through the storms, trials, and prosecutions of everyday life when we decided to accept Jesus Christ as our personal savior. Get prepared by praying, reading, studying, and living by the word of God. The test will come.

In times of family conflict, relationship conflict, financial burdens, loss of employment, church conflict, and times of confusion, how we respond in such situations will reflect what we believe. God does not get the glory from the things that don't happen to you. God gets the glory from the story of how he delivered you through your trials and difficulties. Your deliverance is to be used to help bring in others to Christ. We don't worship God because of what he can give us, but we worship him because he is God almighty. People who don't believe in God, life on earth is what they look forward to. It is not surprising that they hunger after money, pleasure, popularity, power, and prestige. We are in the world as Christians to bring in the harvest, not to become like the harvest that we are in pursuit of.

31 So do not worry, saying, 'What shall we eat?' or 'What shall we

drink?' or 'What shall we wear?' 32 For the pagans run after all these things and your heavenly Father knows that you need them. 33But seek first his kingdom and his righteousness and all these things will be given to you as well."
Matthew 6:31-33

Concerning sexual sin, many churches are very limited to what they teach in the pulpit and in their ministries. Of course every message can't focus on sinful behavior, but people who follow Christ must understand that you can't have an intimate relationship with God, and consistently live a sinful lifestyle. We can't be concerned with offending people who come to church and may not like the message. We must worship God in spirit and in truth. Many people are coming to church to gain a better understanding of the meaning of the Word of God. Some pastors may dedicate two minutes of a sermon to sexual sin then retreat to a broader, safer topic.

There are people who attend church every Sunday, but have sex with people they are not married to throughout the week. Sexual sin can cause major damage to the body of Christ. Sexual temptations are difficult to battle because they are appealing to the normal and natural sexual desires that God has given us. God ordained marriage to provide us with a way to satisfy these natural sexual desires and strengthen this covenant against temptation. Sexual abstinence before marriage is a lifestyle that single people must live if they are going to teach and preach about it. Similarly, fidelity is how married couples must live if they are going to teach and preach about healthy marriage. It's a tough road to walk, but when making the choice to become Christians, it is understood that there will be difficulties.

SINGLES IN THE CHURCH

Every church should create and support a singles ministry. I have had the opportunity to speak at many churches, and very few invest in the singles ministry. I get a lot of calls to speak to youth groups at churches concerning sexual abstinence. When I ask the leadership about the singles, I am often informed that youth are more in need of the sexual purity message than single adults. Wrong! Where do you think youth learn about sexual behavior? They learn from adults! Youth pay attention to adults. It's easy to focus on youth when you want to address sexual perversion. A teenager is more likely to get caught in sexual sin because they are still living at home with their parent or parents. Adults living on their own are free to have sex anytime they want and don't have the worry of getting "caught" by man, but God sees everything.

Consensual sex between adults is not against the law in the United States. After teenagers graduate from the youth ministry, many churches don't do much to keep the ministry going for young adults who become older single adults. Many churches are blind to the fact that they have older struggling singles sitting in their church seats. There is a need to address problems, and challenges of older singles. Church leadership must be active in discussing these issues. I believe many church leaders have forgotten the challenges of being single. Let's be honest, many of our church leaders got married at a young age or became church leaders after they got married. Many of them were not sexually pure during their single lives. Some church leaders may find it difficult to discuss living a lifestyle they did not live, or are not currently living. Whatever the reason, now you are in leadership so keep it real. Leadership must have an open dialogue with singles concerning sex, and not stick its head in the sand and ignore the problems.

I know we are going through some difficult times, so I urge you to build your own personal and intimate relationship with our Lord and Savior Jesus Christ. Ideally, most church leadership would like for everyone to be married, but that's simply not reality. When you are single at any age, God's expectations is that you remain sexually pure until marriage. All singles are not single for the same reason. There are singles who have never been married, divorced, widowed or may not feel called to be married.

There is nothing wrong with being single until you are ready for marriage. Don't let parents, friends, pastors, lust or even loneliness push you into marriage. Being single is the greatest opportunity to build a better you and to provide more service to God. Marriage and being single are gifts from God, and one can be as beneficial as the other. It is important to accept our present status because both lifestyles are valuable to accomplishing God's purpose. Now is the time to prepare yourself for your future spouse. It's never wise to start preparing for marriage just before you approach the altar.

In 2009, Reuters News reported that doctors are failing to diagnose HIV in older patients. They are exposed to greater risk of infection as erectile dysfunction drugs offer extension of their sex lives. This study, published by the World Health Organization, also found that there were increasing numbers of sexually active people age 50 and older who are more likely to risk unprotected sex than younger people. These are single older people who may be divorced, widowed, no children at home, and now they want to explore their options. There are also adults who are allowing tough economic times to influence them to make some unwise decisions. For example, there are professional women who are applying for employment in the adult entertainment industry through films, magazine, and even strip clubs. When things get difficult, we can't subscribe to situational ethics. Regardless of the circumstance, we must stand on the Word of God.

26 At that time his voice shook the earth, but now he has promised, "Once more I will shake not only the earth but also the heavens."[e] 27 The words "once more" indicate the removing of what can be shaken—that is, created things — so that what cannot be shaken may remain. 28 Therefore, since we are receiving a kingdom that cannot be shaken, let us be thankful, and so worship God acceptably with reverence and awe, 29 for our "God is a consuming fire." Hebrews 12:26-28

The old saying "there is nothing wrong with the church, but the people in it" is a truth we must work to change. Some people in the body of Christ seem to have forgotten that we all have made mistakes and bad choices. We must do a better job at showing compassion to all of our brothers and sisters in Christ. To be clear, compassion does not mean to condone or compromise. There are people who are afraid to speak to fellow Christians and church leadership about their struggles. We have the responsibility as Christians to show the compassion of Christ and to help others turn from sinful behavior. We are not to judge our fellow brothers and sisters and allow their situations to become the gossip of the church fellowship. The church should be a spiritual hospital where people can come and get healing for any spiritual, emotional or physical sickness.

These are some very difficult times, but we must stand on the word of God and speak the truth in love. Pastors are responsible for teaching the entire word of God with compassion in order to help people abandon the ways of sin. Times are too serious for the church to lose its prophetic voice by teaching a "watered-down" version of the gospel. We are at war and responsible for bringing in the harvest.

ABORTION

The church must take a more active role in the prevention of abortion. According to the Guttmacher Institute facts and statistics on abortion, there have been at least 46 million abortions since 1973. This was the year that abortion became legal as a result of the United States Supreme Court decision in the case of Roe vs. Wade. Nearly half of pregnancies among American women are unintended, and 4 in 10 of these are terminated by abortion.

There are thousands of women in church who have either had or are thinking about having an abortion. We must provide wisdom through the Word of God to prevent abortion while showing compassion and offering council to women who have aborted children. Abortion would not be an option if people would subscribe to sexual abstinence before marriage.

Fifty percent of U.S. women obtaining abortions are younger than 25. Thirty three percent of women are between the ages of 20-24, and teenagers represent the remaining 17% of abortions performed. Pastors must preach and teach why sexual abstinence and purity is the best option for singles. There are singles sitting in church pews wondering how sex between two consenting adults or teens can have negative results.

CONDOMS IN CHURCH?

Many churches don't teach sexual abstinence or even discuss sex. In 2009, the HIV and AIDS Network of the United Church of Christ recommended that condoms be handed out at places of worship. This is a group within the United Church of Christ, not the denomination as a whole. There are, however, many members and churches within this denomination that do not agree with handing out condoms in places of worship. The HIV and AIDS Network is teaching that condom distribution would save the lives of young people. Jesus saves, not condoms! This is the wrong message for any church to send. It promotes sex outside of marriage as acceptable and okay with God. This is happening because of many church's refusal to deal with and teach the truth about sex, which is an extreme example of taking God's grace for granted.

The church can no longer stick its head in the sand and ignore the problem like nothing is happening. It's time for the church to get serious about dealing with these issues in the church. It's time to be honest and teach the entire word of God. Some members may get angry and leave, but the truth will set you free. Honesty is the best policy.

PORNOGRAPHY

A major struggle for a majority of men and women in our society is sexual sin. Pornography is a lustful activity that involves trying to fill a legitimate need in an illegitimate way. Many men of all ages are addicted to pornography. It provides men and some women with a false sense of reality. In relationships, the needs for men and women are different. Men need respect, recreational companionship and sex. Women need love, conversation and affection. This is the reason that men can become addicted to pornography while a majority of women aren't interested or find pornography disgusting. There are also women who watch pornography, and are working in the adult entertainment industry. Many of these women are in this business for one or more of the following reasons: financial, affection, love, or to be desired. It's a false sense of reality to believe that these emotional needs can be met with positive results from this type of lifestyle.

Many men are introduced to the illusion of sex at an early age through X-rated magazines and/or movies. Addiction can begin at an early age with pornographic images found in X-rated magazines and/or movies. The more men watch these movies, the more they create a false sense of reality to the worth of a woman. Pornography will entice a man look at a woman as a collection of body parts to be lusted after and used. Pornography can also cause men to develop unreasonable sexual expectations of women. Single men who watch pornography have an expectation of how they want their future wife to look, dress and perform in the bedroom. Men get these expectations from their experiences by watching pornography and engaging in pre-marital sex. Married men and woman who are addicted to pornography are emotionally and spiritually cheating on their spouse by relying on another source to fill a legitimate sexual need. Marriage will not cure your lust to watch pornography.

There is a need to engage men by focusing on the issues with which we struggle. Many of our churches are full of women, but the men are few in number. The church must engage men on how to be better men in the eyes of our Lord and savior Jesus Christ. Men are not as emotional as women in a church environment. As pastors stimulate the emotional side of women during Sunday sermons, the same must be taught through biblical factual analytical application for men. We don't care how you dress, sing, hoop, or what you drive, just teach the entire word of god.

MASTURBATION

The end result of watching pornography will eventually lead to masturbation. Many Christians are unclear, don't know, or don't care that masturbation is idol worship and not pleasing to God. The act of masturbation involves sexual fantasies created in the mind to pleasure oneself physically. One may say "What harm can it be, I'm not hurting anyone."

"I am the LORD your God, who brought you out of Egypt, out of the land of slavery.3 "You shall have no other gods before me.4 "You shall not make for yourself an idol in the form of anything in heaven above or on the earth beneath or in the waters below." Exodus 20:2-4

It is impossible to masturbate without lusting. Lust is trying to fill a legitimate need in an ill legitimate way, and is sinful. Sexual Lust is a continuous dwelling thought on a sexual act, and masturbation is an action of sexual lust. I know its deep, but we are to find pleasure in worshiping and pleasing the Lord. Masturbation is about pleasing self, with the object in your mind that you have decided to worship and place before God. In our singleness we are married to God in spirit. We are not to be sexually impure with anyone before marriage, including ourselves. As I began to seek a more intimate relationship with God to help advance the kingdom, I could not be any assistance to God while watching pornography and engaging in masturbation.

Can I be real with you? When I made the choice to stop having sex before marriage it was a battle. My battle was not only with the past fulfillment of watching pornographic movies, but also with the visions of my sexual experiences. I would relieve the sexual lust and tension through masturbation. I stopped having sex, but the memories of my not too distant past still held me in bondage. Pornography and soul ties kept me in a lustful state, which was still sexual immorality and not pleasing to God. I made the decision to start living sexually pure, because I did not want my future relationships with women and my future wife to suffer. Sexual abstinence is an action, but sexual purity is a lifestyle. Temptation will always be there, but your response is important to your growth. I no longer respond to sexual temptation through sexual intercourse, pornography or masturbation. To God be the Glory!

10 Finally be strong in the Lord and in his mighty power. 11 Put on the full armor of God so that you can take your stand against the devil's schemes. 12 For our struggle is not against flesh and blood, but against the rulers, against the authorities, against the powers of this dark world and against the spiritual forces of evil in the heavenly realms. 13 Therefore put on the full armor of God, so that when the day of evil comes, you may be able to stand your ground, and after you have done everything, to stand. 14 Stand firm then, with the belt of truth buckled around your waist, with the breastplate of righteousness in place, 15 and with your feet fitted with the readiness that comes from the gospel of peace. 16 In addition to all this, take up the shield of faith, with which you can extinguish all the flaming arrows of the evil one. 17 Take the helmet of salvation and the sword of the Spirit, which is the word of God. 18 And pray in the Spirit on all occasions with all kinds of prayers and requests." Ephesians 6:10-18

LIVING ON THE "DOWN LOW," A DESTINATION TO DISASTER

When I mention the term "down low," I am not only referring to men pretending to be heterosexuals while having sex with other men. This phrase also applies to anyone who secretly puts others in risky situations, whether physically, emotionally or spiritually. We must begin to address and open our eyes to the sexual behavior of promiscuous, adulterous, and unfaithful men and women in relationships. There are countless people who have lost their families, employment, business, church affiliations and good reputations due to the mindless and perverted pursuit of sexual pleasures.

It is extremely important to develop an intimate relationship with God. Be very careful with whom you allow to occupy front row space in the auditorium of your consciousness. Most people are on their best behavior during the dating stages of a relationship while others have no shame in their game and don't hold back. If someone is honest with you about their freaky and/or selfish behavior, cut them loose! Don't make the mistake in believing that you can change or save someone. Leave that to Jesus. Use wisdom and discernment to weed out the "serious" from the "curious" potential mates.

There are countless stories where men and women have gone through heartache and pain with someone because they refused to end the relationship. This is why sexual purity before marriage is important. While sexual abstinence does not prevent you from having your heart broken, refraining from sex will help you live a lifestyle of spiritual purity. It also provides a clear mind when assessing the assets and liabilities of a potential mate.

Altering your lifestyle to secretly hide anything that you are ashamed of is considered living on the "down low." People who live double lifestyles aren't the only ones with hidden agendas. There are also men and women who are in relationships, but are secretly having sex with other men and women. Some have sexually transmitted diseases and refuse to inform their sexual partners. There are adults who are having sexual relationships with teens. Not to anyone's amazement, this sinful behavior is also happening in our churches among members and leadership. If you don't agree, monitor the day to day news stories of the local and national media.

When making the choice to follow the word of God, there will be tests. God does not lie, and if you follow his word, it will never fail you. The danger of having sex before marriage is the experience of temporary pleasure without concern or caution of penalty. You are only concerned with the pleasure that sexual experience is giving you at the time. As previously stated, one of the three reasons God created sex was for it to be enjoyed between husband and wife without repercussions. A sexual relationship between married couples should be guilt-free because they belong to one another. After sexual intercourse, a husband and wife won't have questions or concerns such as:

- Does he think I'm promiscuous because I slept with him?
- Is she going to want a committed relationship?
- During the "heat of the moment" I made some promises I can't keep.
- We should have not crossed that line. How will this affect

our friendship?
- I feel guilty teaching Bible study after what happened last night.

AT THE CROSSROAD

Sex before marriage can cause spiritual, emotional and physical damage to the individuals involved. Satan is crafty and understands that the immediate pleasure of sexual sin will cause a person to do things that are abnormal. You must never forget that his goal is to steal, kill and destroy you and your seed. The benefit of all sin is immediate gratification without care or concern until negative consequences develop. This is a reason why sex outside of marriage is specifically causing a major problem with our youth and singles. Many problems in the Old Testament were caused by the worship of idol gods. This worship was mostly to Ashere and Baal idols that encouraged and commanded sexual perversion. These heathen religions promoted sodomy, lesbianism, fornication and bisexuality.

Satan, knowing the weaknesses of men and women, used sexual enticement and perversion to get them to disobey God. His goal is to steal, kill, and destroy so he would never inform us about the dangers of living a sexually immoral lifestyle. He knew the instant pleasure of sex would influence people to ignore the problems of sex outside of marriage. Satan has and will continue to only promote the selfish pleasures of sex. Today, the only thing that has changed is the appearance of the idol. Many people are living in sin because they worship and lust fame, money, cars, homes, security, men, women, lust and much more. Much of the behavior that is being displayed by today's youth is a byproduct of what has been taught by adults. Many of these persons living this dangerous lifestyle may have been a victim of abuse. Some have been molested, raped or emotionally and/or physically abused during some period in their lives. Due to these negative experiences, many people struggle when it comes to their sexuality. They lack capacity to love or to be loved and often fail to trust any form of affection. These issues are in turn brought into relationships and marriages that usually end in resentment, pain, abuse and even divorce.

If you are reading this book and are involved in "Down Low" activity, please repent, and rededicate you life to God. The greatest gift God gave us outside of Jesus was freedom of choice. We can no longer allow someone, something or some bad experience cause us to make decisions that are potentially harmful to us and others. We have the freedom to make choices that will be a blessing to us and the God we serve.

As a young boy, I was molested by a male babysitter whom my parents trusted. I knew something was wrong with the way he touched me, and the things he wanted me to do. I dreaded going there, but one day I got angry and informed him that I was going to tell my parents. His actions stopped, but I never told my parents. I was afraid, confused and embarrassed about telling my parents what happened. I harbored this anger in my spirit for a long time. After this incident I never questioned my sexuality, but now I know and understand why many men and women do after going through similar situations. During those years of my life, I was having major problems in school and was always getting into trouble. I made the promise to myself that one day that when I became stronger, I would kill the babysitter who molested me.

It wasn't until I joined Eastern Star Church in Indianapolis, Indiana, at the age of 23 that I rededicated my life to Jesus and forgave the babysitter, and turned him over to the judgment of God. I am blessed that my parents never gave up on me and played a major part in helping me become the mighty man of God that I am today. I love my mother and father with all of my heart. They are almost a perfect example of what parents should be. I am blessed that they chose each other to bring me into this world.

I made the choice to forgive and to move forward with what God had planned for my life. For others, it's not that easy. There are many people living on the "down low" because of similar negative experiences they had during their adolescence or "not too distant" past. If your excuse for "down low" behavior is due to your past, get some help. Let it go, and move into your destiny that God has ordained for you.

Apostles Peter and Judas made bad decisions in similar situations. Peter told Jesus that He would never leave him, but later denied that he knew Jesus three times. Judas conspired with the Jewish counsel to betray Jesus for money causing Him to be captured and crucified. The difference is that Peter repented of his sin, and continued with God's plan for his life by preaching the gospel of Jesus Christ. Judas allowed guilt and condemnation to drive him to suicide. This is an example of two similar situations with two different choices and results. I thank God I was able to forgive and move towards my destiny. Please don't allow temporary pleasure, past hurts or confusion provide you with a lifetime of pain. Free will allows us to choose the path we will follow, please choose wisely.

CONCLUSION

LIFE LETTERS AND "WORDS OF WISDOM"

Growing up can be a pain
You're not an man until you come of age
We've given up our teenage years
In the effort to pursue our career
Who assumes responsibility
Of having to support our families
Who's protecting us from harm
Is there anyone around
That we can trust

So we search for answers to our questions
Looking for a answer
No answers but we're taught a lesson everytime
Through mistakes we've learned to gather wisdom
Cause lifes responsibility falls in our hand oh

Keep on learning
Keep on growing
'Cause wisdom helps us understand
We're maturing
Without knowing
These are the things that change boys to men

BOYS TO MEN
Lyrics "Boys to Men"

"With such nagging she prodded him day after day until he was tired to death. So he told her everything. "No razor has ever been used on my head," he said, "because I have been a Nazirite set apart to God since birth. If my head were shaved, my strength would leave me, and I would become as weak as any other Man." *Judges 16:16-17*

"Having put him to sleep on her lap, she called a man to shave off the seven braids of his hair, and so began to subdue him. And his strength left him. Then she called "Sampson, the Philistines are upon you!" He awoke from his sleep and thought, "I'll go out as before and shake myself free." But he did not know that the Lord had left him. *Judges 16:19-20*

BOYS TO MEN

As men we are responsible for setting a standard for the growth and development of our families, which include our wives, our children, and ourselves. Sexual immorality has been a major problem for men since the beginning of man's existence. Again, I want to thank the many married and single women who have preached, taught, and spread the message of sexual purity for all single males and females regardless the age. It is time for men to "Man Up" and make the necessary psychological, emotional, and spiritual transformation from "Boys to Men" concerning sexual purity.

As men, we must take the responsibility in helping our boys understand the characteristics and responsibilities of Godly men. Regardless of past and present mistakes, we have a responsibility to impart wisdom to our young men. We want to make sure they have the necessary tools to pass the test they will encounter during their lives. They will and must be tested and it is our duty to help prepare them as much as possible. Our present and future families depend on the relationships we have with our women of God. We must continue to remind ourselves as men, and teach our young men that:

- Making babies outside of marriage does not make you a man, it makes you irresponsible
- It's responsible to pay child support and spend time with your children, but it's wise to refrain from sexual activity until marriage to raise your children in a two parent home without the "Baby Momma Drama"
- Using a condom does not protect you from all sexually transmitted diseases
- Using a condom does not protect you from the emotional and spiritual consequences of sex (obsessive behavior like stalking women)
- Females are to be loved and respected, not looked at as objects of desire to be used and abused. How would you want a man to look and treat your mother and sister?
- Choosing a wife will one of the most important decisions you will ever make
- Godly married men don't cheat on their wives, and single men don't cheat in their relationships
- We gain wisdom and discernment by having an intimate relationship with God by praying, reading, studying, and living by HIS word.

Young men who are irresponsible learn their behavior from

irresponsible adult men. These men don't understand that action speaks louder than words, and young men often duplicate the actions they see. There are adult men who are responsible and engaged in their son's lives, and others whom are involved in youth programs. We have many men who are working with youth to eliminate gang violence, drug use, and promote the benefits of a quality education.

The few men, who speak to young men concerning sexual activity, limit their words of wisdom to the use of a condom and "safe sex" practices as the only form of birth control. The men who provide this ill-advised solution are single men who engage in premarital sex, and married men who engaged in sexual activity before marriage. Men who speak up for God and sexual purity are looked at by many as square, ignorant, foolish, and promoting a lifestyle that is impossible for men to live by.

Who says men can't be sexually pure until marriage? Who says men can't be faithful to women in committed relationships without being sexually active? Who says men can't be faithful to their wives in marriage? The only men who feel this way are single men who engage in sexual activity, the women they are sleeping with, and the married men and women who cheat on their spouses.

Godly men know in spite of our past mistakes, we are "God Chasers" who are not perfect but have a burning desire to please God by feeding the "Spirit Man" and not the flesh. Let's be honest with our young men and share with them some of the unwise choices we may have made in the areas of sex, drugs, fighting, lying, cheating, and any other negative actions God delivered us from. We can't allow pride and a false perception of perfection (now that we are doing better at living a life pleasing to God) to hide the fact that we all make mistakes, and to seek forgiveness from God, our women, our children, our family and friends is what Godly men do.

6 Train a child in the way he should go, and when he is old he will not turn from it. Proverbs 22:6

It's time for "Men of God" to break the manly "Code of Silence" and speak life, wisdom, and Jesus into the lives of our future men, husbands, and leaders. Let's remind ourselves and teach them:

- Block out sexually impure thoughts by redirecting your focus to something positive and non sexual like sports, starting a business, or going to subway
- Not to become weak and drop your guard because women

respect and admire you
- Learn to appreciate the beauty of women, but learn not to lust after women
- Be cautious and prayerful of the type of women you love, give affection and conversation
- Before passion grows, decide what type of woman you will love
- Determine if a woman's character and faith in God is as attractive as her beauty
- Sexual purity will allow you the opportunity to make sure a woman's personality, attitude, and commitment to solve problems are as gratifying as her hugs
- The enemy will attack when you are emotionally and physically drained, so get proper rest
- You must be tested, so study the word of God to prepare yourself
- Be patient, no need to rush

14 Do not worship any other god, for the LORD, whose name is Jealous, is a jealous God. 15 "Be careful not to make a treaty with those who live in the land; for when they prostitute themselves to their gods and sacrifice to them, they will invite you and you will eat their sacrifices. 16 And when you choose some of their daughters as wives for your sons and those daughters prostitute themselves to their gods, they will lead your sons to do the same. Exodus 34:14-16

Always stay alert to the schemes of the enemy. We can never pray enough, read the word enough, or attend too many church services. Don't take "sinning breaks" (you know what I'm talking about "Lord I've been good for 3 months, so I deserve a little break") because the enemy is looking for a crack to launch his attack. Please be cautious of what type of women you allow to occupy time in the auditorium of your mind. God created women to be loved by us, and for her to be a helper suitable for us. Choose your helper (wife) wisely, because every woman you meet does not have the intention to help. It doesn't make you less of a man to run from temptation. Run my father, my brother, my son. Run, run, run, and run!!!!!!!!!!!!!

10 And though she spoke to Joseph day after day, he refused to go to bed with her or even be with her. 11 One day he went into the house to attend to his duties, and none of the household servants was inside. 12 She caught him by his cloak and said, "Come to bed with me!" But he left his cloak in her hand and ran out of the house. Genesis 39:10-12

The enemy understands the plans that God has for men to help advance his kingdom. Working and ruling with our women in dominion to rule the earth is his desire for us. The journey of being Godly men is a never ending process, but how successful the journey will depend on the choices we make. Choose life. Choose Jesus Christ as your King.

Love, peace, and eternal happiness.

Darren L. Washington

HEAVENLY HELP DURING THE HOLIDAYS

One of the most exciting or possibly depressing times of the year for singles is the holiday season. It all depends on whether you look at your cup as "half full" or "half empty." During Christmas season, we spend time with family and friends and celebrate the birth of our Lord and Savior Jesus Christ. Thanksgiving, Valentine's Day, birthdays and other so-called holidays are also challenging times for singles in search of relationships. These are also times when many singles' vulnerability to sexual sin heightens.

Many of us see engaged or married couples and those in relationships enjoying various holidays. In addition, singles endure pressure from family and friends with statements and questions such as "You are such a great catch. I can't believe you are not married," or "When are you going to get married so I can be blessed with grandchildren?" Questions like these can cause one to ponder the possibilities, your choices, future and most important, how you see "your cup." This self examination will consist of your past, present, and possible relationships. Jesus is not concerned with our past as much as He is focused on our possibilities. Forgive, but learn from past mistakes, and shape your present in order to create a promising future.

When we indulge in sex outside of marriage, we sin against our bodies that belong to God. We are also called to glorify God in body and spirit. God also does not want us to be driven by our selfish desires and lust, but calls us to be holy and pure. He puts this call on our lives because his holy spirit dwells within us. We cannot have intimacy with God while having sexually immoral relationships.

As singles we must desire companionship with God through an intimate relationship. We must consistently read His word, believe His word and act on His word. Talking and listening to God and seeking his mind and heart will aid us in identifying His will for our lives. Especially during the holidays, the thought of sex begins with a need to feel accepted, loved, feel beautiful, be close to someone, be respected or feed lustful desires. Do not allow a temporary circumstance to possibly cause a lifetime of discomfort. Lust is trying to fill a legitimate need through illegitimate means.

I am not saying that abstinence will always protect you from a broken heart, but abstinence better equips you to deal with a broken heart. It is also better than having to deal with the stress of a sexually transmitted disease, unwanted pregnancy, guilt feelings, condemnation, anxiety, damaged self-esteem, loneliness, disappointment, depression, doubting salvation, family breakdown, abortion and soul ties. I know it may be difficult to hear, but the truth shall set you free.

When making the decision to start over, you must be willing to "die" out to some things in life so that God can take you to the next level. This includes everything that is keeping us from an intimate relationship with God. We must be willing to take up our cross and God in order to be worthy of his goodness.

Are you willing to make the necessary changes to please God? Are you willing to cease sinful activity in order to get closer to God? He created male and female to dominate the earth and rule together in dominion. We as men and women of God should not dominate one another. If we were so valuable to God that He would send his son as an offering to die for our sins, can't we "die" to the things that are preventing a closer, intimate relationship with Him?

Be encouraged, especially during all holiday seasons, to strengthen your relationship with God. As singles, look at your cup as full because as mighty men and women of God, we are worth the wait. We now have the opportunity before marriage to get our spiritual, physical and financial house in order to be a blessing in the marriage covenant. I pray that your faith doesn't fail during the holidays because God is ready to take you to the next level for His glory. Don't concern yourself with finding "Mr. or Mrs. Right." Be prepared when God brings him or her into your life.

"Weakness is not sin, but using your weakness as an excuse to sin is sinful and unwise."

Love, peace, and eternal happiness.

Darren L. Washington

MARRIED IN OUR SINGLENESS

Have you ever been in love with someone? Have you ever been in love with someone who did not love you the way you loved them? Have you ever been in a relationship where the other person was unfaithful, and no matter what you did, it was never enough to make them love you and be faithful? Today, many single Christians are sitting in church every Sunday, going to Bible study while committing adultery against God. We are called to live a life of purity in body and spirit until we meet our spouse. We are married in our singleness to God and must remain faithful to Him.

There are few times in the Bible where God makes an attempt to help us understand through human example how he feels. God loves us but is displeased and hurt when we continue to live a lifestyle of disobedience. In the book of Hosea, God provides us with an example through the marriage of Hosea and Gomer. Israel adulterous lifestyle and unfaithfulness towards God is revealed.

> 2 When the LORD began to speak through Hosea, the LORD said to him, "Go, take to yourself an adulterous wife and children of unfaithfulness, because the land is guilty of the vilest adultery in departing from the LORD." 3 So he married Gomer daughter of Diblaim, and she conceived and bore him a son." Hosea 1:2-3

If you have ever been hurt in a relationship by an unfaithful person, this is how God feels when we are unfaithful to Him by not obeying His word. God instructed Hosea to marry a woman with whom he would fall in love and would be unfaithful to him. It's easy to be in a relationship where you are reaping the benefits, but you are not "in love" with that person. God wanted Hosea to understand how much it hurts when the person you love does not love you based on their actions. As singles, we have a responsibility to be faithful to God in our marriage to Him. Living outside the word of God is adultery. Faithfulness to God is the perfect training ground to help singles prepare for marriage. You can't be faithful in marriage to God if you are:

- Having sex before marriage
- Watching pornography
- Practicing masturbation
- Engaging in oral sex
- Engaging in any type of sinful activity

God loves us, but we can't build an intimate relationship with Him while engaging in these activities. God is a loving and forgiving God. It is a blessing that God's ways are not ours otherwise we all would have died a long time ago because of our sinful behavior. No matter what is in our past, God is always willing to take us back, but we must be willing to live in submission to His will.

1 The LORD said to me, "Go, show your love to your wife again, though she is loved by another and is an adulteress. Love her as the LORD loves the Israelites, though they turn to other gods and love the sacred raisin cakes."

2 So I bought her for fifteen shekels of silver and about a homer and a lethek [b] of barley. 3 Then I told her, "You are to live with me many days; you must not be a prostitute or be intimate with any man, and I will live with you."
Hosea 3:1-3

After everything Gomer put Hosea through, he still took her back. This time, he had to buy his wife back by paying a price for her! Hosea had a legitimate reason to divorce his wife, but he stayed because he loved her. He did, however, lay down certain conditions. She could no longer be a prostitute or be intimate with any other man. God loves us so much that He sent his only son to die on the cross, shed his blood to become a sin offering for the world so that we might be saved and have eternal life. Based on our unfaithfulness, God could have given up on us a long time ago.

I pray that "A Dummy's Guide to Sexual Purity and Dating" will assist you in your desire to become more intimate with our Lord and Savior Jesus Christ. This book is not only about sexual purity, but about keeping pathways open to hear from God and accessing the benefits of the Kingdom while winning souls to his Kingdom. Enjoy marriage in your singleness. It's an awesome experience!

Love, peace, and eternal happiness.

Darren L. Washington

WORDS OF WISDOM

1. Be careful of becoming a "Best Friend" to a person of the opposite sex. When a single man and a single woman have this type of relationship, someone will eventually want more.

2. Men, be honest with women from day one. They may not like what you have to say, but you will gain their respect, and you will put the ball in her court to be responsible.

3. Ladies, when a man is honest about what he wants from you, don't make the mistake in thinking you can change him.

4. Men who are dogs are not born this way, they are created by silly women.

5. Don't waste your time dating someone whom you know could never be your husband or wife. Release them so that their focus won't stay on you but rather what God has for them.

6. It is easy to be friends with someone to whom you are not attracted. When you meet the person that makes your heart skip beats, this is where the friendship must begin.

7. It is not wise to be friends with someone who is in love with you when you know that you will never feel the same.

8. Never fill your desire for intimacy at the expense of another person's heart.

9. Never spend your time trying to convince someone why they should be with you, when they don't want to be with you. I know it's hard, but let go and move on.

10. Ladies, we make time for things that are a priority to them no matter how busy we get.

11. Ladies, the Bible says "When a man finds a wife, he finds a good thing." Don't waste your time chasing men because the men you chase are not looking for you anyway.

12. Marriage is so much more than sex, so keep yourself sexually pure

so you can make an adequate assessment of the qualities a person can bring to your potential marriage.

13. God is not going to choose your spouse. He loves us too much by giving us "Free Will" to make that decision for us.

14. We are free to choose between sin and righteousness, but we don't have the authority to manipulate the consequences of our choices.

15. You are ready for a dating relationship when you don't need to have a dating relationship.

16. Men, be careful and prayerful where you plant your seed. All soil is not good ground.

17. Age is only a number, so don't lower your Godly standards to get married.

18. Most men fall into sexual immorality because of lust, and most women fall into sexual immorality because of loneliness.

19. Women, be careful of the men you allow to give you conversation, affection, and love.

ABOUT THE AUTHOR

Darren L. Washington is a native of Gary, Indiana and a 1988 graduate of Horace Mann High School. He earned a Bachelor of Arts degree in Political Science from Millikin University in Decatur, Illinois and a Master's Degree in Public Affairs from Indiana University Northwest.

Darren's early interests in youth, community service and politics were nurtured as an intern for the United Way of Central Indiana where he developed and coordinated the first Youth Leadership Program and during the 1996 legislative session where he served as an intern for the Indiana State Senate.

His tenure as Executive Director of the Indiana Commission on the Social Status of Black Males included working with state, county, and local elected officials to create city and county commissions in the cities of Gary, Evansville, South Bend, Muncie, Anderson, Michigan City, Fort Wayne and Lake County Indiana. He also coordinated four state conferences, published three annual reports and developed two publications on issues concerning the Black Family.

After three years with the commission, Washington made his transition to corporate America working in Real Estate Investment and Telecommunications. While his time in the corporate sector provided him the opportunity to further develop his management skills, it lacked the opportunity for self-fulfillment and gratification in giving back to his community.

When the opportunity to "come home" and make a difference presented itself, Darren accepted the challenge by returning to Gary, Indiana. In 2004, Mr. Washington was elected to serve as the At-Large member of the Gary Community School Board of Trustees, and serving as President during his first term. He is known in the community for launching the GO! "Back to School Campaign." This grassroots effort involves volunteers canvassing and knocking on the doors of Gary residents, encouraging parents to join the PTA. Washington's many awards include the 2005 Millikin University Young Alumnus of the year Award; he has also received the key to the cities of Evansville and Muncie, Indiana.

As a state certified HIV/AIDS prevention counselor, he speaks to thousands of youth and single adults on the issues of relationships and sexual purity. Mr. Washington has been the subject of televisions news stories, newspaper articles and has appeared in magazines such as "Being Single", "Spiritual Perspective", "Christian Single", "Essence", and "Jet" concerning his views on education, sexual purity and family values. He has also been a guest on the BET television talk show "Let's Talk Church" hosted by Gospel Legend Dr. Bobby Jones.

Mr. Washington is also the host of his own radio and cable television shows titled "Singles in the City" which air weekly in Northwest Indiana. You can also live stream his programs on www.singlesinthecity.tv

"For this reason, since the day we heard about you, we have not stopped praying for you and asking God to fill you with the knowledge of his will through all spiritual wisdom and understanding. 10 And we pray this in order that you may live a life worthy of the Lord and may please him in every way: bearing fruit in every good work, growing in the knowledge of God, 11 being strengthened with all power according to his glorious might so that you may have great endurance and patience, and joyfully 12 giving thanks to the Father, who has qualified you [a] to share in the inheritance of the saints in the kingdom of light. 13 For he has rescued us from the dominion of darkness and brought us into the kingdom of the Son he loves." -Colossians 1: 9-13

CANVASSING FOR CHRIST

As an elected At-Large member of the Gary Board of School Trustees in Gary Indiana, I must appeal to voters citywide. My strategy has always been to walk door to door, and speak to residents as to why I should represent them as a member of their local school board. This strategy allowed friends, family, supporters, and myself the opportunity to speak with voters concerning my qualifications and accomplishments.

During the 2008 presidential elections we saw people in masses going door to door in their neighborhoods to support specific candidates. We also saw people who believed in these candidates so much, they traveled anywhere from one hundred to one thousand miles to coordinate campaigns and go door to door in other cities.

One day while studying the word of God, the Holy Spirit asked me a question: Why won't Christians go door to door and campaign for me? "I have the solution to every problem, because my yoke is easy and my burden is light." As singles we must become actively involved with bringing in the harvest.

The mission of Canvassing for Christ is to use Christian Citizens of God's Kingdom to go out among the masses and spread the good news of salvation, through the gospel of Jesus Christ. We will carry out this mission through the following goals:
- Canvassing door to door in residential neighborhoods and public establishments;
- Working with churches and organization already spreading the gospel through door to door;
- Praying with and for residents the prayer in Colossians 1:9-13;

- Leaving residents with information that can help assist with personal needs;
- Giving residents a New Testament bible to help encourage the reading of God's word; and
- Preparing for canvassing by increasing our prayer life.

Our consistent prayer is to have all Christian churches to encourage their membership to go out door to door and spread the good news of Jesus Christ. I believe church attendance and membership would increase if we went out and brought in the harvest.

If you know of any church or organization that can donate bibles for this campaign, please contact me. We are using the "Holman Christian Standard New Testament Bible" at a cost of .50 cents per bible. If you would like to donate to this campaign you can give through my website, or mail donations and bibles to:

Singles in the City
P.O. Box 892
Gary, Indiana 46402

"Then he said to his disciples, the harvest is plentiful but the workers are few. Ask the lord of the Harvest, therefore, to send out Workers into his harvest field." Matthew 9:37-38

ABSTINENCE IS AN ACTION BUT SEXUAL PURITY IS A LIFESTYLE

Visit or contact the following for additional information.

SINGLES IN THE CITY
Darren L. Washington, CEO
Speaking Engagements and donations to
support "Canvassing for Christ":
darren.washington@sbcglobal.net
singlesinthecity@sbcglobal.net

INTERNET ADDRESS
www.darrenwashington.com
www.singlesinthecity.tv
www.dw-singlesinthecity.blogspot.com

"Lord it is my prayer of faith, and I touch and agree with the person who has read this book that they understand your will for their life, they gain spiritual wisdom, they please and honor you Lord, they bear good fruit through their works, they grow in the knowledge of your word, they be filled with your strength, they have great endurance and patience, they stay full of your joy, and they always give you thanks in the name of our Lord and Savior Jesus Christ."

SPECIAL THANKS

DR. MICKY BEACH

PASTOR ROOSEVELT BRADELY

CHARLIE BROWN

STACY BURNSIDE

DR. MYRTLE V. CAMPBELL

DEBORAH DELK

JUDY DUNLAP

PASTOR PHIL ENDRIS

RAGEN H. HATCHER. ESQ

TIYANE Q. MIKE

DAWN PALMORE

AMI REESE

MERARI SANTIAGO

DR. VERNON G. SMITH

MARK SPENCER

SARITA STEVENS

WILLIE STEWART

ANTHONY THIGPEN

PASTOR CHRISTOPHER THORPE

CHELESA L. WHITTINGTON

LaVergne, TN USA
16 April 2010
179513LV00004B/2/P